W9-ATS-950

The Sea Wall

BY EILÍS DILLON

BELL BOOKS

The Sea Wall

Illustrated by W. T. Mars

FARRAR, STRAUS & GIROUX   NEW YORK

Library of Congress catalog card number 65-17024
First printing, 1965

Printed in the United States of America
Designed by Jean Goodrich

The Sea Wall

For as long as John could remember, old Sally had been talking about the big wave. She always began on it in the late spring, when the days were getting sunny and warm and when all the whitewashing on the island was about to begin. As soon as she saw the first kitchen tables piled high with crockery, standing before the open doors, she was reminded of that terrible spring so many years before.

"The whitewashing was just finished, inside and out," she said to John. "There wasn't a house in Inisharcain where you couldn't hold a wedding, or a station, or a funeral. Then one evening, about six o'clock, there was the wave looking over the sea wall at me."

John shivered, though he had heard the story of the wave so often before. He was sitting on the hob by Sally's fire, waiting for her grandson Pat, who was his great friend. Sally's house was the last on the quay road, the short road that led downhill to the island's little pier. It was the nearest house to the sea, and the people used to say that this was why she feared the sea so much.

"Neighbors are never too fond of each other," said old Tom Faherty. "Doesn't the world know that?"

Tom himself had no neighbors. He lived alone in a little house which was so high on the cliff that its thatch had to be held on by an old fishing-net. Else it would have blown off in the first winter storm and left him like a crab without a shell, inside.

Yet Sally was not really afraid of the sea. She had her own boat, a canvas-covered currach in which she went fishing and collecting seaweed for her little garden. No other woman on the island dared to do this. The boat had belonged to Sally's husband, and after he died she had refused every offer to buy it. Every spring she repaired it and tarred it with her own hands, until this year when at last Pat was old enough to do it for her.

"Go on about the big wave," said John.

"If it looked at me, I looked back at it," said Sally, "and I said in my own mind: you're up to no good."

And she went on to describe how the wave had spilled over the wall, and had come racing up the road with herself racing before it to warn everyone that it was coming.

Then there had been the agony of time lost while the people took in the news. Old Mrs. Hernon had been the worst. She was eighty-seven then, and a great-grandmother, and as deaf as a beetle. Her son shouted to her that the wave was coming.

"Shave?" she said. "Why? Is there a funeral? Are you trying to break news to me?"

He tried again.

"Your daughter? Which one? Why don't you call her by her right name? Haven't you six daughters?"

"Water, Mother! Water!"

At this point Sally had seized Mrs. Hernon and hauled her to the door and pointed.

"A wave!" said the old woman. "Why didn't you tell me? We'll have to gallop."

And she hitched up her skirts and galloped, for the first and last time in twenty-five years, as she said herself.

Such destruction as that wave had done! When it had gone back to its own place, the houses that it had visited were full of sand and seaweed and shells, and even a few dead fish. Crockery was broken, featherbeds and pillows ruined, doors lifted off their hinges, thatch holed and sodden. It would break your heart to see it, Sally said. And yet, a great blessing, not a single life had been lost.

"God was good to us," said Sally. "He sent that wave for His own good reasons, whatever they were, but He picked a good time for it. Six o'clock was perfect. The men were all home from the fields and the bog, the children were all home from school. The mothers were all cooking. Every family was together and that's how it should always be in times of misfortune."

So the whitewashing had all to be done again and it was many months before the signs of that wave were gone.

"But they forgot it after a while," she said. "You'd think people would never forget a thing like that."

"It's a long time ago," said John.

"Twenty-nine years this spring," said Sally. "That seems a long time when you're young, but as you get older it's only like a few months. They think it will never come again. But I say that what happened once can happen twice. Often and often my James told the people that the sea wall would have to be rebuilt. He said that if the wall had been high enough, the wave would have spread out wider, and it would never have come up the island the way it did. He was knowledgeable about those things, from working on the big dam in Australia when he was young. But sure, no one would listen to him."

"Why not?" This part of the story was new to John. "Isn't it always wisdom to listen to a man that's talking sense?"

"I think they thought he was boasting about all the traveling he had done," Sally said after a moment, "or else it was another thing."

"Go on, Sally. What other thing?"

"Even to say it is a terrible thing," Sally said, "but I've often thought that if one life had been lost, we'd have our new sea wall this many a year."

"Did you ever say that to anyone? To Tom Faherty, or to my father?"

"No. I know it's foolish to be superstitious, but I had a feeling that it should never be said. It would sound as if I wished someone had been drowned in that flood, to save the rest of us."

"If you said it, though, you might frighten the people into doing something about getting the wall rebuilt," said John.

" 'Tis true for you," Sally said. "But I'm thinking it may be too late now."

"Too late? What do you mean? The new wall can be built any time."

"Come outside for a minute," Sally said.

John followed her out into her little front garden. It was not much bigger than her kitchen, but it was a beautiful garden, with a low whitewashed wall between it and the road. Round white stones from the nearby shore edged its single path. On either side of the path there were heavy-scented wallflowers, alive with bees. Just as John reached the door, in through the bar of the little gate came Sally's huge black cat. The sun shone on his fur so that he looked as if he had been polished. His green eyes were round with excitement and his whiskers bristled. Across his mouth, so that it looked like a moustache, he carried a mouse.

"Just in time," Sally said. "This is what I wanted you to see."

The cat laid the mouse at her feet and went to rub himself against her legs. She looked down at him with pride.

"That's the finest cat on the island," she said, "and a sensible cat. If you were out here a minute ago, you'd have seen him coming down the road there, from the cross, bringing home the mouse."

"Down from the cross? Why?"

"Because there isn't a mouse to be found from the cross down, for the past month."

"He's a great cat, indeed," said John.

"It isn't that he has caught them all," Sally said. "It's how they all moved away from here. And the cats too. My cat is the only cat on the quay road now, and even he won't sleep in the house any more. Up on the thatch he goes. Every house I go into when I do be rambling around here in the evenings, there isn't a cat to be seen, hair nor hide of one. Hannah Fagan thinks my cat frightened them off, but I know better. And I'll tell you another thing: for twenty years the swallows are nesting under my thatch. This year they didn't come at all."

"Perhaps they're afraid of the cat," said John.

"It couldn't be that," Sally said positively. "Haven't I always kept a cat? The cats know, and the birds know, that that wave is coming again."

"How could they know?"

"That's more than I can tell you. They know it the way the beavers know in America when the bad winter is coming, and build their houses high. They know it the way the birds know when a volcano is going to blow up, and clear off to a safer place. My James saw these things and 'twas he told me. If he were alive now, I know what he would do."

"What can anyone do? It would take a hundred bags of cement to mend the wall that's there, not to mind building a new one. And every bag of cement would have to come out from Galway on the steamer. If those cats are right—"

"Now I frightened you," said Sally. "Sure, I didn't

mean to do that at all. And still a person would have to be a bit foolish not to be frightened of that wave I saw the day long ago. It was like seeing a dragon out of one of the old stories come prancing up the road."

"What would James do, if he were alive?" John asked, wanting to quench the light of terror in her eyes.

"He'd write a letter," Sally said. "A letter to the County Council in Galway. He could write like a bishop, God rest his soul. In that letter he would remind them of what the wave did before, and he'd write it in such a way that the cement would be landed on the quay and the work begun a week later."

"Why don't we write a letter?"

"Long ago I would have written it, if I were able." She laughed suddenly. "I had great times when I was young. I had two big brothers, and everything I did was what they wanted to see me do. When they went out in the currach fishing or cutting weed, I was with them. When they went to the bog, they were never contented unless I was there too. They took me to Galway to the fairs, over to Connemara to all the weddings, out to Aran in the summertime to visit our cousin there. A fine time, indeed, and not a day ever but once did I darken the door of school."

"You did go once?"

Sally turned back into the kitchen and settled herself on the hob, gathering up her long red skirt so that the fire could warm her shins. She gave a little chuckle.

"Once I went to school, sure enough," she said. "I was delighted going. I had a new red dress and a white apron with white embroidery around little holes on it, that my mother brought me from Galway. I had a white ribbon in my hair too. Five years old I was. The teacher was a man from the County Clare, across there where the blue mountains are, that I'm looking at every day since I was born. He was as tall as the church steeple, I thought, and as thin as the oar of a currach. I went with Mary Peter. She was ten years old and very sensible. I was fond of Mary and I would have stayed in school if I could have sat with her. But *mo léir!* She had to go off and leave me, and sit with the big ones at the other side of the school, and there I was on a small little bench by the door. There was a nice little girl sitting beside me, and she had on a new dress too, and a white apron with embroidery, and a big white ribbon.

" 'Where do you come from?' I asked her, and I put out my hand, I remember well, and touched her apron to see was it the same as my own. She had lovely brown hair, curly and soft.

" 'From Casla,' she said.

" 'We'll meet after school and we can play,' I said to her.

"But with that, didn't the teacher call out to us with a voice like a foghorn, God bless him: 'No talking allowed! Stand over there by the door, the two of you!' He was a decent, kindly man, as I found out afterwards, and he had sweets in his pocket for every one of us, but while I was standing there by the door, I couldn't get the thought out of my head that when school would be over, he was going to kill the two of us. The door was open, and the larks were singing outside because it was not long after Easter. I looked out and saw my brothers walking down to the sea carrying the currach. I didn't wait another minute but darted out through the doorway and off down the road flying. I never went back to school after that, though the teacher used to be calling at the house every second day for an age, trying to get me to come. I used to run off and hide when I'd see him coming, and my poor mother used to have to listen to him. And that's why I can't write a letter to the County Council in Galway, because I can't read nor write at all." She picked up the tongs and set to arranging the fire. "I hear you're a great little scholar," she said.

"I go to school every day," said John, "if that's what makes a scholar."

"Staying away doesn't make one anyway," said Sally. "I never missed the skill of writing before. We'll make a letter, between the two of us."

She had a pen and paper because Pat used to write regularly for her, to her son in America. She got these out and laid them on the table.

"I didn't ask Pat to do the letter for me," she said, "because I know he hasn't come to letter-writing yet, at school."

"But doesn't he write to America for you?"

"Yes, yes, he does. But this must be different. It must be a fine, dignified letter, the kind you'd learn to write in school. Start off there, now, and I'll be watching you and making the tea for the two of us at the same time."

In the top, right-hand corner, John wrote: "Inisharcain, Galway Bay." Then he wrote at the left-hand side, lower down: "The Secretary, The County Council, Galway." That looked very well. Under it he wrote: "Dear Sir."

All of that was in the school book, but not a word more,

not a single mention of sea walls, nor great waves, nor bags of cement. In the book, what usually followed was a request for a certain amount of goods to be sent and charged to an account. This was not much good now. Seeing that he had paused, Sally said:

"What are you stopping for? Why don't you get on with the letter?"

"I must think."

He began to get a prickling pain in his forehead while he tried to work it out: please send one hundred bags of cement and twenty strong men and charge them to my account. What would they make of that, in Galway? Sally was very quiet about making the tea, not wishing to disturb him. But he could see the disappointment growing in her face as she glanced at him from time to time. At last, in desperation, he wrote very quickly:

"Dear Sir: Twenty-nine years ago a great wave like a dragon came prancing up over our island. By the mercy of God no one was drowned. We know another big wave is coming soon. Our sea wall is broken since the last one. Please send cement and men quickly or we may not be so lucky next time. Yours sincerely—"

"Whose name will I put on the end of it, Sally?"

By this time she was looking very happy. She was cutting and buttering a mountain of soda-bread. She paused with the knife held high.

"What name? Sure, we must put a name."

"I could put your name," John suggested.

"No. A woman's name would be no good. It must be a man's name or they won't come. You could put your own name."

"They'd be raging mad if they were to come all the way out here and find it was a boy had brought them."

"We could put Tom Faherty's name, maybe."

"But if you were to do that, you'd have to tell him, because they might write to him. I know what I'll put: S. MacDonagh. S stands for Sally, but they won't know whether it's a man or a woman that wrote to them."

She was delighted with this arrangement. When the letter was sealed and stamped, they settled down to get through the soda-bread. In the middle of it, Pat came in.

He was a year younger than John. He had been out on the mountain after sheep and this had given him a fine appetite. Very soon, Sally had to work on the loaf again. When he was partly filled, Sally said:

"I was telling John what I told yourself, that I know another big wave is on its way, God protect us all! So he wrote a letter asking the County Council to send at once to mend the wall for us. The post boat will be here tomorrow and they'll surely get the letter the day after. They could have the men out working on the wall in a week's time if they send an engineer to look at it immediately."

Reaching for another slice of bread, Pat said:

"Did you say in your letter how you know there is another wave coming?"

"We did not, then," said Sally, "for they would only laugh at us. City people don't ever want to believe those things. We can tell them when they come, of course. It would be different when they would be here. They might believe then that there is sense in those signs."

"I didn't rightly believe in them myself until this evening," Pat said. "I separated the goat from the sheep and took her from the mountain with me, as we said."

"Has she a fine bag of milk with her?" Sally asked eagerly.

"She has, faith."

"I'll go out in a minute with the can and get it from her," said Sally.

"That's what I want to tell you, that you'll have to go up to Donnelly's yard to milk her, for I couldn't move her a step beyond the cross. I had the rope around her horns and she came along, nice and quietly, until we got to the cross. Then she lifted her beard and opened her nostrils wide and rolled her eyes around like a Christian. She planted her feet there, and not a move could I get out of her after. I pulled her and I shoved her, but 'twas no use. In the end, Mrs. Donnelly came out and said I could leave her in the yard until she'd get a bit of sense. But I'm thinking now it's not want of sense is on her at all, but too much of it."

"God help us all," said Sally. "That wave is coming for certain sure."

The same evening, the boys went down to have a look at the sea wall. It was a beautifully calm evening, with the sea a greenish blue, as smooth as silk. One could hardly believe that somewhere in it a monstrous wave was hiding, waiting for a chance to swallow up the island. At the edge of the sea, inside the shelter of the quay, the waves broke with a short, sharp sound as they rolled the tiny colored shells about.

They went down there first, to collect handfuls of these shells, which were a delight to have in one's pockets. They were all colors, purple and yellow and red and brown, and a bigger kind that was grey like a pearl. Afterwards they walked along the curve of the quay and looked down from above at the sea wall.

It had been built long ago of boulders, huge and square, filled in with concrete to form a solid barrier. From the continual battering of the sea the concrete had worn away so that great raw patches showed, through which the foundation rocks were visible. Here and there, the sea had lifted the rocks out of position and had tumbled them down in a little avalanche. Through the clear water they could see these rocks, which had once been a part of the wall, now lying in dark, weed-covered patches on the sea's sandy floor. Where they had been, great holes gaped.

"Every year those holes get bigger," Pat said. "It's through them that the wave will get its chance, when it comes."

Neither of them wanted to look at it for long. They soon turned away and went up the cliff path to visit old Tom Faherty. It was John's idea.

"If the Council sends out men, it would be as well not to have the people that will meet them looking too surprised. Maybe we could make Tom a bit uneasy about the state of the wall."

When they reached Tom's house, at first there was no one at home but his old sheep-dog, lying as usual in the ashes at the edge of the fire. From living alone, Tom had become a careless housekeeper. His dog was no better. He was too old to run out and meet visitors on the doorstep, and he had developed a habit of wagging his tail in welcome, where he lay among the ashes. This sent a cloud up to settle on the china dogs and on the mantel clock above, so that everything up there was coated with ashes. The walls of the kitchen had not been whitewashed for several years, and they were broadly stained with brown from the puffs of smoke that came down the chimney in stormy weather. Soft drifts of ash moved under their feet as they went into the kitchen. A moment later, Tom came in.

"Visitors! I found two short tea-leaves floating in my cup this evening, and sure enough, here come the visitors."

He offered them a pull at his pipe, but they knew better than to accept it even if they had wanted to. Tom's pipe was an aged clay. As John said afterwards, he would as soon suck at a sod of turf as at its blackened stem. In any case, they had both given solemn promises not to smoke until some far-off time when they would be grown men.

Tom pushed the dog away from the fire and pulled out two creepie stools which he dusted with his cap. Then he sat on the hob and began to poke among the ashes for the seed of the fire. He built a little wall of turf across the back of the fireplace, placed the red coals against it, surrounded it with a ring of sods and then began to fan it with his cap. At once a little feather of smoke began to drift up the chimney. The motion of the cap sent more ashes out into the room. Tom took no notice. He was watching his fire with a delighted expression.

"Look at that, now! Seventy-nine years I'm living in this house and never once did the fire go out on me. I suppose the day it does, I'll be on my way to heaven. Tell me, now, how are they all below at the quay?"

"They're starting the whitewashing," said John.

"Ah. 'Tis the time of year for it, sure enough. My own

place could do with a touch." He cocked his head on one side. "What day of the week have we?"

"Friday."

"No school tomorrow. Couldn't you two fine heroes come up tomorrow and do a bit of whitewashing for me?"

"We could, but there's more than a day's work in it."

" 'Tis true for you. It gets worse and worse on me, and I never noticed it. Sunday is a day of rest. Monday afternoon, after school, you can start again."

This was agreed and then Tom said:

"You can tell Sally I'll be down for my dinner on Sunday and maybe on Monday and Tuesday too, for I won't be able to boil the spuds with the whitewashing going on."

Everyone knew that Tom never boiled a potato but lived on bread from Donnelly's shop since his wife died five years before. He was always ready with an excuse to visit someone else's house at dinnertime, therefore. No one grudged him the meals they gave him. A visitor brought a blessing on the house, they said, and besides, they might be in the want of the same charity themselves one day.

"We were down looking at the sea wall before we came up here," said Pat. "It's in a bad state."

"You've been listening to your granny," Tom said at once. "She's never done talking about that wall. It will do our time, I'm always telling her. Isn't that good enough for her?"

"What about *our* time?" John asked indignantly. "Don't we matter at all?"

"Sure, I'm only joking," Tom said apologetically. " 'Tis

a fine sea wall. Not a drop comes over it, the worst storm we ever have."

"You wouldn't think that if you lived below on the quay," Pat said. "After a storm, I'm often able to gather enough weed to manure a garden of cabbage."

"Sure, that happens everywhere," said Tom, "and isn't it grand and handy for you to find the weed on your doorstep instead of having to go out in the currach for it?"

"One of these days we might have the fishes handily swimming into the kitchen so that we won't have to go out after them either."

Tom laughed, but he looked a little more uneasy.

"Of course, Sally is afraid because she was the first to see the big wave the day long ago. I was working away in Clifden at that time and I never saw it at all. I'm always telling her that if you live near the sea, you'll always be thinking it might forget some day to stay where it belongs."

Still, for all his light talk, they thought they had put a doubt into his mind about the safety of the wall. On Sunday when he came to Sally's house for dinner, he strolled down the quay and had a look at it himself. Pat and John went with him, though they were drowsy from dinner and from their labors of the day before in Tom's kitchen.

Several of the men who lived in the neighborhood were at the quay already, leaning on the wall in the sun, pulling at their pipes. Mike Fagan, who was Sally's nearest neighbor, called out to Tom:

"I hear you have two fine painters up at the house these days."

" 'Twill be like a palace when they're finished," said Tom. "We'll have a party."

He climbed stiffly up the flight of stone steps that led to the top of the quay and stood there looking out over the sea. Mike followed him anxiously.

"What brings you up there at this hour of your life? Come down out of that, Tom, or you'll fall for certain sure."

"When I didn't fall the other five thousand times I was on this quay, I won't fall now," said Tom. "I came up to look at the state of the sea wall."

" 'Tis easily seen where you had your dinner," said Mike. "Look at that wall. Not a stone has stirred in it this twenty years."

"They have, and stirred," said Pat indignantly. "There's a new fall of rocks from the storm in January, and the end of it, over there, fell off in March—"

"Those are little things," Mike said impatiently. "You're getting like a little old woman, so you are. 'Tisn't natural for a boy to be always with his grandmother."

"I can see for myself," Pat began, but he stopped then because he could not think of having an argument with a man of Mike's age. In any case, neither of the men would have listened to him. They were talking to each other about the prospects for lobster fishing that summer, and they seemed already to have forgotten about the whole problem of the safety of the wall.

But three days later, when they saw the pilot boat approaching the quay, they were ready enough to take charge of everything. Long before the boat reached the quay, they were down there waiting for it.

"What is bringing them out at this time of the year?" Mike wondered.

Roddy Hernon peered at the boat, which was still too far away to have its passengers identified.

"There's two strangers on it," he said. "Maybe it's the new doctor from Bofin, wanting us all to get vaccinated against one of his germs."

"What germ would come to Inisharcain, I'd like to know?"

"Maybe it's the veterinary inspector to count our bulls and our stallions."

"*Ochón ó,* I hope it isn't the veterinary inspector!"

No one wanted it to be known how many animals he had, not even how many dogs.

"Five shillings for a dog license! 'Tis a mint of money to pay for a dog that might be no good at all. Maybe the men are coming about the dog licenses."

"Or maybe they're Civic Guards, to watch every move we make in and out with the currachs, to watch every little fight between neighbors, that would be made up in a week or two anyway."

"Maybe it's the inspector for the school. It's certain sure the thin one is an inspector of some sort or size."

"Maybe they're coming about pensions."

This was said by little Stephen Cooney, the tailor, who was the only one to see a brighter possibility.

By this time the boat was near enough for them clearly to see the tall, thin stranger in his fine suit. Suddenly Mike recognized the fat man that was with him.

"It's Andy Phelan, our own County Councillor," he said, jumping around in his excitement as his habit was. "Now what in the name of all that's wonderful is bringing Andy Phelan out here at this time of year, and no election coming?"

No one could think of an answer to that. They waited for the boat to come alongside the quay, catching the ropes that the crew threw ashore and making them fast to the stone bollards. The thin man sprang on to the quay without help, but Andy Phelan had to be hoisted ashore by the pilot and his mate, like a sack. He stood on the quay at last, panting and sweating.

"Good day to you all," he said heartily. "I'm not used to boats, as you see, but I'm always glad to come to Inisharcain."

There was no one rude enough to ask him why, in that case, he did not come more often. Though he represented several of the islands at the County Council, it was well known that he cared little or nothing for the people that lived on them. It was not his fault, the islanders said charitably. To know and understand the islands, you had to be born and brought up on them, or at least to have lived on one of them for a number of years. When some great problem came up, the priest who came every Sunday was consulted, or the teacher. No one would have thought of asking Andy Phelan to get the post boat to call more often, or to visit a sick person in Galway Hospital, or to write a good letter about a pension.

Watching him standing there on the quay, with his big false smile, John said quietly to Pat:

"Why do they elect him every time, I wonder. Look at him! What does he care about our sea wall, or if this whole island were washed clean of its population tomorrow—"

"We can't judge by looks," Pat said doubtfully. "Maybe

he's good-hearted enough. Look at the thin man," he added suddenly. "They've come about the wall, for sure."

The thin man had already climbed onto the top of the quay and was looking down at the wall. Slowly he walked along, and he seemed to be surveying every inch of it. Andy pointed up to him with pride.

"He's an engineer, Mr. Lynch. We came all the way out from Galway to let you know how anxious we are about your welfare."

"Ha!" said the pilot boat's mate loudly, and spat into the sea.

"Yes, indeed," Andy said blandly, straddling with his legs and rolling up and down while his voice developed an echo like a ship's siren, "to let you know that while we lie snug and warm in our beds in Galway, we are always aware, always conscious of you out here in the wild Atlantic, in daily frightful peril."

"He's hardly on dry land before he begins to make a speech," said Pat in disgust. "Come on up and we'll fetch down Sally, or all we'll get out of this visit will be a mouthful of talk."

As they turned away, they heard little Stephen Cooney angrily answering, and they paused for a moment to listen.

"There's no call for you to come all the ways out from Galway to insult us and our island, Mr. Phelan. The last time I was in Galway there was a hurricane that took the slates off of one half of the houses, and yourself and the likes of you were shivering in your beds for fear the wild Atlantic would walk in the door to you."

"Now, now, I meant no offense," Andy said hurriedly.

"Come on," said Pat impatiently.

They ran up the quay and arrived panting in Sally's kitchen just as she was taking a loaf of bread out of the pot-oven.

"Andy Phelan and a long string of misery, Mr. Lynch that he says is an engineer, are below on the quay. Go down, quickly, or it will all go wrong on us after all."

"Take the loaf, then," said Sally. "Wrap it in the clean cloth there on the window—"

She was off out the door, leaving the hot loaf in Pat's hands. Somehow he got it onto the table without dropping it. Then, with John's help, he wrapped it in the cloth, very carefully, and immediately it began to steam. They set in on the window sill and darted out of the house again, and ran after Sally.

She had already reached the quay by the time they got there. At once they saw that by now all the men were furiously angry. Stephen Cooney's voice was as sharp as a sea-gull's as he shouted:

"And Mr. Phelan, if we were to catch yourself and your Mr. Lynch and fire you over the quay wall, it might be the best way of showing you that you can't come out here in your steamer and make little of us because we live on an island. Sure, isn't the whole of Ireland an island, if it comes to that?"

There was a note of desperation in Andy's voice as he answered:

"I didn't mean to make little of you. I only said I have the problems of the poor nearest to my heart—"

"Who are you calling *poor*?"

This was Roddy Hernon, in a threatening growl. Mike Fagan said in the same tone:

"You'd best not use that word to us again. 'Tisn't because we have to ask you to do a thing for us now and then that you have the right to insult us. There isn't a man, woman or child on this island ever goes hungry."

Sally slipped in front of the men and said quickly:

"Look, Mr. Phelan, 'twas very nice of you to come out with your engineer to look at the wall. As you see, it's in bits, and 'twill have to be mended. And there's another big wave coming, I know, for the animals and the birds are afraid to come down on the quay and that's a sure sign—"

"And from this on, the County Councillors will be afraid to come onto the quay either," said Stephen Cooney. "Our quay wall is all right. We don't want any strangers coming around here, looking down on us, making game of us, insulting us."

"It's in a dangerous state," Sally said loudly. She spoke up to the engineer who was standing on the wall above, looking down at the men and listening to what they were saying. "Mr. Lynch, you're a man of knowledge. Wouldn't you say that wall is in a dangerous state?"

The engineer nodded.

"You see!" Sally turned triumphantly to the men. "I'm right. It will have to be mended at once, before the big wave comes—"

"Stand aside, Sally!" said Roddy Hernon. "This is no place for women. Don't mind her, Mr. Phelan. She's ramaishing about that wall since I was in petticoats. Now let me tell you something." He dropped his voice and said in a soft drawl: "We'll give you one minute to get onto your boat and get started on the long voyage back to Galway. If you're not on that boat inside of one minute, we'll be able and willing to help you."

All of the men moved two steps forward, lightly and silently. Andy Phelan looked at them in astonishment and then in terror. Mr. Lynch sprang down off the quay wall and thence onto the deck of the pilot boat, still without uttering a word. Then, with a little moan, Andy followed him, as awkward as a cow on the little ladder that was set in the quay wall. With one flick of their hands, two of the men threw the ropes on board. Immediately the pilot boat drifted a yard away. The pilot and his mate grinned at each other, as if they had enjoyed their little interval at the quay. Then they got the engine going, and with a friendly wave to the crowd of men standing on the quay, they set off for the open sea.

"Good riddance of bad rubbish," said Stephen Cooney. "We won't see that bold hero in these parts again for a while."

Sally and the two boys moved away. The old woman looked as if she were going to cry.

"If I could have got the two of them up to my kitchen and made them a cup of tea, with a piece of my fine new soda-cake, we could have talked reason. Stephen Cooney was never a day at sea in his life. What does he know about what the sea can do?"

" 'Twas Andy Phelan that ruined everything," said John. "From the minute he put his foot on the quay, he was saying the wrong things."

"With grown men, that shouldn't matter," Sally said impatiently. "I pray God I'm wrong about the big wave."

But Sally was not wrong.

For days afterwards the men went about their work with growls and grunts.

"The poor! That's the sort of talk that goes down well with city people, maybe!"

"We gave him 'poor,' so we did."

"He won't be around again for a while, I'm thinking."

"I'm afraid they're right there," John said. "Andy Phelan got the fright of his life that day. One good thing was that he never said a word about the letter."

"He didn't have time," said Pat.

"If he had mentioned that letter, I'm thinking you and I would be buying our passage to the New World by now."

The days were warm and sunny, and it became very hard to sit all day in school learning how to calculate profits on the Stock Exchange, and what were the chief exports of South America, and why the French Revolution happened. The school door stood open, and tantalizing sounds came in as clear as bells on the light air. The clanking of a cart could be heard on its way to the beach for sand, and the voices of the women as they washed their beloved crockery in great tubs outside their doors before putting it back on the kitchen dressers. All the whitewashing was done; all the doors and mantels were painted with red paint, picked out in white. In a few weeks the fat cabbage roses would be in bloom. Already the strong, exciting smells of seaweed and wallflowers and newly-growing grass filled the air, so that even the teacher looked restless. It seemed as if the sea would always be calm and the air always full of the songs of birds and the ticking of grasshoppers, right through the whole long summer.

Then one day there was a sharp little wind. It sprang up at about midday and within a few minutes it had changed the sea's color from a silky green to a blue that was like ink. On the far western horizon, away where there were no more islands, a bank of white cloud appeared. It spread wide and high during the afternoon, with jagged points on top, until it looked like a range of mountains. Waves began to roll in onto the white beach behind the quay. One by one the men went down to move their currachs up higher.

" 'Twill blow off to-morrow," said Roddy Hernon positively, "but it might make a bad night. That's a fierce lot of cloud to the west."

Old Sally trotted down to the quay when she saw Roddy and Mike there.

"You may as well move my currach too, as you're at it," she said.

"To be sure we will," they said. "We'll move yours first and we'll move our own after."

They lifted Sally's currach between them and got in under it, carrying it upside down so that it looked like a huge black beetle with long legs. When they were ready to move, Sally said:

"I want you to bring it up to my own house for me."

They had taken the first steps but they stopped dead when they heard this.

"Why?" Mike's voice came hollowly from inside the currach. "We'll leave it up on the grass here, and weight it well on each side with stones the way the wind won't lift it—"

"It's not the wind I'm fearing at all, but the sea," said Sally sharply. "I feel it all over me that this will be the night for the big wave. If I lose that currach, I'll never have another one as long as I live."

Roddy laughed.

"But the last time there was a big wave, it came up to our house and away beyond it. Didn't I often hear how my grandmother ran from it and she eighty-seven years of age? If we put the currach above at the house for you, sure the wave will take it just the same."

"I know," said Sally. "I know that very well. But if I had it at the house, I'd put a rope on it the way when the flood will go down I'd have my boat still, or the carcass of it. And if I lose it, I'll have the satisfaction of seeing what happens to it, maybe. 'Tis only a short little walk," she finished coaxingly. "If I could do it myself, I wouldn't ask a sinner to help me."

The men made no reply to this. They lifted the currach and followed her up the road to her house, planting their feet carefully and steadily. Just out from school, John and Pat came down the road together and met them. They stood and watched her directing the men how to lay the boat on the ground against the little garden wall. This was done in complete silence. The men brought stones to prop the boat and to weight it down, and then they walked off, back to the beach, with only the shortest word of farewell.

"What's got their tongues?" Pat said to Sally.

"It's the way they think I'm gone cracked in my old age." Sally laughed but she seemed angry. "What can I do? I feel it all through me that the big wave is coming with this storm. I told them that, and that I want my currach where I can see it. I wish they would move their own boats too. 'Twill be a terrible thing if the wave takes all the boats." She looked the two boys over sadly. "I can tell by the looks of you that you think I'm cracked too. Well, maybe I am. I'll be glad if you're right. Let you go down now and see what are the men doing with their own boats and I'll have the tea made when you come back."

They could not look at each other as they walked down to the strand. It was true that they thought bringing her currach to the house was the strangest thing that Sally had ever done. And yet they could not help believing her. They shivered as they went down to the beach. There was a whistle in the wind now and the waves had grown huge. They reared their heads high like prancing horses and then dropped suddenly onto the strand with a sound like thunder. Broken seaweed darkened the water, and every wave threw some of it onto the beach, so that now the white sand was spotted with brown. Jets of spray shot into the air at the sea wall.

The men were gathered by their boats, talking quietly. As the boys came near, Mike raised his voice.

"Well, she may be wrong or she may be cracked, but I'm bringing my currach up home tonight too."

"And I," said Roddy. "I won't sleep a wink for thinking of it, if I leave it down here. I'd rather have the labor of bringing it up to the house and have my night's sleep after."

There were five hookers moored at the quay, too—big, black, wooden boats with sails—but there could be no question of moving these. In any case, they were not in such danger as the currachs. The men knew that, being heavy, the hookers would just sink to the bottom of the little harbor. They could easily be refloated afterwards. But if a high sea were to take the currachs, they would just disappear, and perhaps a few splinters of their fragile frames would be washed in, days later, as the only sign of what had happened to them.

One by one, the men began to say:

"No harm in bringing the currachs up a bit of the way."

"It's going to be a fierce storm, even if there's no big wave going with it."

"It's better to be sure than sorry, when it's a question of a boat."

"We'd look fine and foolish if she turned out to be right."

"We'll look fine and foolish if she turns out to be wrong, too, each of us with a boat outside his door, like Noah."

"We'll look foolish anyway, it seems, so we may as well do the safe thing."

And after some more of the same talk, one and all they brought their currachs home. Pat and John helped with two of them. They met in Sally's kitchen afterwards to talk about it.

"You should have seen Hannah's face when she saw Mike bringing up the currach and leaving it against the house wall," Pat said. "She came running out to know what was the matter with it. He told her he wants to tar it in the morning, and that he'd like to have it near home to be handy for boiling the tar on the fire."

"Mrs. Moran was told the same thing," said John, "but she looked out and saw all the boats coming up the road and she said it must be because of the storm. So her husband had to tell her it's going to be a bad night and he thought the boat would be safer. There will be great praying going on in all the houses this evening, I'd say."

"Maybe if they pray hard enough, the wave will be sent

some place else," said Sally, and then she added quickly: "But I wouldn't wish it on anyone, God between us and all harm."

"Are you so certain that wave is there?"

"I'm not certain, I suppose," Sally said, "only that the evening feels the same as it did long ago. It was a spring tide, like this evening, and the same high bank of cloud was there. And the strangest thing of all was that a shoal of some queer fish came in to the quay, big grey fish that their like was not seen around here before or since."

"I saw those fish this evening," said John. "They were behind the sea wall for a while, a big patch of them, like the shadow of a black cloud. Then they were inside the quay for a while. The men were watching them, and dying to go after them, only most of the boats were gone, and anyway the sea would frighten you."

There was silence for a moment and then John said eagerly to Sally:

"Let yourself and Pat come up to our house for the night. Pat can come in with me and you can have the settle bed by the kitchen fire. You'll get a great welcome from my mother—"

"Don't I know that, a-mac," said Sally. "Your mother's welcome is fit for a king. But I never slept a night out of my own house in fifty years, except for the time of the last wave. Haven't I got Patcheen, here, to keep me company?"

"Pat's company won't be much good to you if the wave comes," John said. "You'd be safe up in our house. You can hardly hear the sea at all, up there."

"Isn't that the trouble?" said Sally. "I'd never sleep if I couldn't hear the sea." She gave a sudden little cackling laugh. "And sure, I'm not as old as Mrs. Hernon was, the night long ago, when she galloped up the hill before the wave. Can't I do the same?"

When it was time for him to go home, John went outside with Pat and helped him to lash the currach to the biggest rocks in the garden wall. Darkness had almost fallen. The sky was so low that it seemed to be about to press down on the island and squeeze the life out of it. Here and there, little points of light darted through the blackness of the clouds. The wind roared all around them with a noise like thunder. From the strand came the terrible din of the stones being rolled about by the surf.

"The tide is almost full," said Pat as they finished the last knots.

They turned at the same moment to look at the sea. Then they saw the wave. There was no mistaking it. It seemed to be about half a mile away. Out in front of it the sea was flat, almost hollow-looking, as if all the smaller waves had drawn backwards to form this one huge monster. It came sailing along, high and proud, and in the first moment when they saw it, it seemed to John to be almost happy-looking. He remembered how Sally had said of the other wave, that it had looked at her. This one seemed alive too, not wicked at all but wild and free and wonderful.

There was time to see all this and to draw one long breath before they were across the garden and standing in Sally's kitchen. It was Pat that said:

"The wave! It's coming!"

Sally just opened her eyes wider. She said not a word but took a quick look around her kitchen. Then she reached up to the shelf above the fireplace, took down the clock with the oak case and held it under her arm. There was no time to think of anything else. They were outside in a flash. Sally closed the door, and gave a little chuckle at the foolishness of it. She glanced down towards the sea and shook her free fist at it, once. Then they were off up the quay road. Pat stopped at Hernons'. As they ran on, the others could hear him shout across the half-door:

"The wave! It's coming! Run, everyone run! Leave everything there—"

They heard no more. Sally trotted into Donnellys', going like an old hen. It was well she was so thin, John thought as he ran on to Fagans' and Connors'. The two houses were side by side. The two fathers were standing inside the kitchen doors. Within a minute, each had got his currach into the kitchen and had his family outside running for the hill. Now came Pat, galloping like a colt to Morans'.

So they went from house to house of those nearest to the sea, looking back on each doorstep to point downhill. The wave was over the sea wall by now and still coming, though it seemed a little less high. At Stephen Cooney's, John saw that Sally's house was half under the sea. There came Sally and Mrs. Donnelly, hurrying Sally's goat between them while the water washed around their ankles. The Morans were driving their donkey, which was going faster than he would ever consent to do at his day's work. The Connors had their sow and her litter of fifteen little pigs, but she was too slow and they had to leave her. All the way up the hill to John's house, Mrs. Connor cried after her sow and her little pigs, lamenting at the top of her voice. John's mother came out to greet her:

"Mary, Mary, are all the children safe? Why are you keening like a banshee?"

"My sow, my little pigs!" said Mary. "They were my store, my treasure, my wish, my whole life!"

"God forgive you, Mary!" said John's mother briskly. "What do they matter when your husband and your children are all safe? Keep your keening till we find out if any Christian lives are lost."

She bundled her in onto the hob, to sit there swaying up and down and moaning to herself, so that as the kitchen filled up each newcomer quickly counted the five Connor children to make sure that she had no good reason for her wailing.

Except for Mrs. Connor, the people were very quiet. The men stood outside, at the gable of the house where there was a little shelter, and watched the sea. John and Pat were just old enough to be allowed to stand with them, instead of being penned into the kitchen with the children. These had already got used to their new situation and had begun to enjoy it with little yelps and shrieks that pierced the ears of everyone but themselves.

Watching them, John tried to remember what it had been like to be five or six years old and to leave every trouble to the big people. He knew that in a year or two each of these same children would be given charge of a flock of geese, or a few pigs, or even of a cow, and that they would begin then, as he had done, to know that when you live on an island everyone's work is important. Five years ago, when he was eight years old, he had had to stay for half the night with the cow that he was minding when she slipped and fell into a drain by the bog road. He could not leave her, and he was too small to get her out. There was nothing to do but wait until his father found him after a long search. The morning after this experience, he was a man.

In the last of the daylight, they could see how the island had suddenly got smaller. Now the sea was at the top of the quay road. It reached just to the thatched roof of Donnelly's shop, which looked like a floating stack of corn. Sally's house, and Hernons', and Connors', and Fagans', had utterly disappeared, with all their sheds and outhouses and garden walls. It was some comfort to know that the boats were safe in the kitchens, but no one could bear to talk of the condition of the rest of their property.

A strange thing was that old Tom Faherty's house on the cliff now stood on an island of its own. The sea had poured into the hollow behind it, cutting it off completely. But Tom had got out before this had happened and was watching as anxiously as anyone, to see if his house was going to be submerged.

Wrapped tightly in her shawl, with one hand clutching her big black rosary beads, Mrs. Donnelly came out of the house. Her husband left the men and came over to speak to her.

"It's stopped," he said. "It will rise no more. All the things are safe. Let you go in now and drink your tea. There's no more to be done but to trust in God."

Fiercely she gazed downhill at the roof of her house. Sally came out and stood beside her.

"It's you we have to thank," Mrs. Donnelly said to

Sally. "I knew you were talking sense. When you said the cats and the mice were all gone away from the sea, and when your goat wouldn't go home any more, I got my man to help me and we put all the lovely things above in the loft on the rafters—the flour, and the meal, and the tea and sugar. All of those things used to lie in their bags on the floor. If the sea won't rise any more, they're all safe. It's you we have to thank for it."

"We'll thank God for it," said Sally. "It won't rise any more."

Still Mrs. Donnelly would not believe it until an inch of the house wall appeared, showing that the sea was going down again. When they saw this, all the men gave a great shout that brought everyone running, not only from John's house but from the other houses around where people were sheltering. In the fierce blast of the wind they stood watching, while little by little the island took on its natural shape again.

John was surprised to see that the wave, which had rode in prancing, as Sally had said, just trickled out quietly, not looking like a wave at all. First came the walls of Donnellys' house, then a piece of their garden wall. After that, the top of the road appeared, running with little streams as it did after heavy rain. Next the roofs of the houses on the quay road showed. A heavy "Oh!" went up from the watchers when they saw the great holes that gaped in the thatch. The sea was much slower in flowing away than it had been in coming. Still it kept moving steadily, gathering in its trailing ends from every hollow, leaving the earth glistening.

At last the curve of the quay wall was seen. Everyone sighed, recognizing it. Often there was a high tide that looked rather like this. It was not so very strange now. The families began to talk among themselves about how soon they would be able to get the houses cleaned, dried, and roofed again.

" 'Tis well the summer is coming," Stephen Cooney said. "There would be a lot of drying in a few breezy days."

The people whose houses had been untouched by the wave began to make sleeping arrangements for their unfortunate neighbors. There would not be enough beds, of course, but with a good turf fire to keep them warm, no one would complain of spending a few nights on a blanket in the kitchen.

No one had had any supper, so the first thing to be done was to hang great pots of potatoes over the fires. Mrs. Donnelly said to her husband:

"Let you go down and bring up a bag of flour and we'll make a few soda-cakes. They'll be wanted in the morning."

She hung her shawl on the peg behind the door and began to help John's mother with her task of cutting and buttering bread for the children. Several of the other women watched her for a moment or two. Then they began to lay the table with cups and plates, so that in a short while it looked as if a great party were about to begin.

It was more than a week before the people could go back to their houses. They could not have gone back even then, if everyone on the island had not worked together to make it possible.

First the hookers had to be salvaged at low tide, where they lay full of water on the sandy floor of the harbor. When they were baled out, they floated as comfortably as they had ever done, though Christy Moran's one had a broken mast. After that, no one did any other work but thatching, except for the necessary things, milking cows and goats and bringing in the day's food.

The weather was dry and sunny after the storm had blown away. This meant that the thatching could be done quickly. Luckily it had been a good summer the year before and there was plenty of straw. Four men worked on each roof. First the old thatch had to be stripped off and the rafters examined for cracks. Sods thick with matted grass roots were laid on the rafters and then the whole roof was thatched with straw. The boys were sent for sally rods to bind the new thatch. All of the men were expert thatchers. The women watched them silently, peeping up at them every time that they came in and out of the houses. It was only when the roofs were on that they began their usual chatting and gossiping again.

For the women, the return to their houses was a torment. Wet straw from the collapsed roofs and wet sand covered everything. The walls that had so lately glowed with whitewash were now a miserable grey. Blankets and pillows were heavy with sea-water. Turf ashes from the soused fires made horrid little smears everywhere. Holy pictures and photographs of the relatives in America were ruined beyond all hope. Cups and plates and dishes were reduced to little pieces, though Sally by shutting her front door had saved a number of hers from destruction.

One great thing was that all the currachs were safe. Every man, as he carried his currach back to the shore, stopped at Sally's door to thank her for saving them. They made sure that her house was the first to be thatched, and day after day the women took it in turns to help her with her washing and cleaning.

"I hope they have learned something," she said to the boys on the first day that she was able to live in her house again. "God knows they've paid for their education. There's Mary Connor with her sow and her little pigs gone, and all the lovely crockery broken, all the featherbeds full of sand that will never be got out of them again, and the whitewashing to be done all over, and the painting. Tell me, now, when the two of you went around the houses, did you hear anyone saying that word should be sent in to Galway about the sea wall?"

"No," said John. "I heard the opposite."

"What did you hear?"

"In Hernons' they said that the last wave came twenty-nine years ago, and the next one will come twenty-nine years from now, so there is no hurry with the sea wall."

"God help us all!"

"And in Connors' they said the same, and that if we had men from the County Council out, the next thing would be that we'd have inspectors looking at everything and counting everything."

"Wouldn't it be worth it? I'd rather have an inspector walking in the door any day than the salty sea. Did they talk about how the sea wall looks now? Have they seen that big bank of white sand lying up against it, that you can see when the tide goes down?"

"Yes, they have all been down to see it."

"And don't they know that that sand will ease the passage of the wave up over the wall the next time?"

"No," said Pat. "They say it will strengthen the wall. They say the wave has repaired the wall for us by filling in the holes and making a fine breakwater behind it."

"That's not how it works at all," Sally said. "My James said that sand is no good for keeping out the sea because it's too easy to move it. You can see that with half an eye, how the sea is always carting sand about and dumping it here and there. Over in Inisheer, hasn't the church and the graveyard and all gone under it, that used to be high on the island? If a wave were to come this way again, we might come down after and find that our houses were full of sand to the roof, so that it wouldn't be worth our while to dig them out, God between us and all harm."

"Could the sea wall be rebuilt by ourselves, without anyone coming out from Galway?"

"No, that could never be done. Maybe if James were here he could direct the work, but I'm thinking even he couldn't do it. It's a job for a man of education, like that Mr. Lynch that was here with Andy Phelan."

When everything was in order again, Sally went to visit all her neighbors and admire the work that they had done. In every kitchen she sat for a while on the hob and drank a cup of tea, and always before she left she said:

"May we never have such misfortune again. 'Twould be a terrible thing if a wave like that were to come again in the autumn. It wouldn't be so easy to clean up everything and mend the thatch and all, with the winter coming on."

By this means she hoped to get the women urging their husbands to send for the engineers to mend the sea wall while there was still time. But her plan went wrong. Everywhere John heard the same thing:

"Because she saved the boats for us, because she was right the last time, she'd be glad if another wave were to come so that she could be right again. Old women always love to be right."

John told Pat about it because of course no one would speak of Sally in this way while her grandson was present.

"That's all the thanks she gets," Pat said furiously. "Now I understand something. That smallest Connor boy, Colie, that's still in a skirt—the one with the long curls his mother won't cut off because she thinks he's such a beauty—"

"Yes, yes. What about him?"

"He called after me to-day: 'Your granny is a crow! Your granny is a crow!' I didn't know what he meant. Now I know that he heard it at home. They think she's bringing bad luck like an old crow, just by talking about the wave that might come in the autumn. Next thing you know, they'll be blaming her for the last wave."

"She'll have to stop warning them, from this out," said John.

They told Sally something of what John had heard, though not all of it. It did not seem necessary to hurt her feelings by letting her know all of what her neighbors were saying.

"So you'll have to give up advising them and let them take their chance," Pat said.

"How can I give up? What about all the Connor children? And the Morans? We've had two warnings and still no life lost—"

"Whatever you say, don't say that," said John quickly. "If there were another wave and if a life were lost, they would call you a murderer."

"It doesn't make sense," said Sally, and there were tears in her eyes from anger and impatience. "Are they just going to sit in their houses waiting for the sea to come and pick them out the way you'd pick a periwinkle out of the shell?"

But something of Sally's warning had taken hold of the people's minds, as the boys found on the first day that they went to the bog. It was a Saturday, the first really warm, dry Saturday since the flood damage had been repaired. One would think that nothing had disturbed the life of the island for centuries, everything looked so peaceful.

The bog was at the highest point of the island and was reached by a long road that led straight up from the cross-roads nearest to the quay. Until nine o'clock, a procession of flat carts pulled by donkeys and ponies clattered up the road. The women and children sat on the carts, their dangling feet brushing the leafy brambles on either side. Everyone was in good humor. The women shouted to each other, questions and news and jokes. The men walked, each behind his own family cart, so that they had to shout too, to be heard by the other men. Larks sang overhead, so high that they could not be seen except through eyes watery from the sun.

High on the island, the air was thin and clear. It was a wonderful place for a bog because when the turf was cut it dried quickly into firm black sods that would burn steadily through the long winter evenings. Each family owned a piece of the bog. A little causeway of stones led off the road into each plot. At these, one by one the don-keys were unharnessed and turned loose to graze on the margins of the road. The big oval baskets of food were set against the old banks of turf, and then the work began.

The men had been at the bog already, a few days be-fore, to cut the turf into long wet sods and lay it on the ground. Now the sods were ready to be footed. They had to be lifted one by one and placed standing on end, four together, with their points leaning inwards, and with a fifth sod laid across the top, so that the sun and the air could get at them from all sides.

At first it seemed like easy work just to pick up the sods and stand them upright, and make sure that they did not fall down again. But within twenty minutes, one by one the children began to creep away, rubbing their backs and their arms which were numb and sore from stooping and from the weight of the turf. No one called them back to work. All of the older people remembered very well what that pain was like. They knew too that as one got older, the muscles needed became tougher and stronger, so that in time one was not troubled by them at all.

At noon the work stopped for an hour. The baskets of food were all brought to a long stack of last year's turf, which gave shelter from the wind, like a wall. Carefully the women spread their shawls on the grass. Everyone sat down, the men leaning their tired backs against the turf stack while the women handed them great slices of buttered soda-bread with bacon. Roddy Hernon made a turf fire on the edge of the road where it could do no harm, and a kettle of water was put sitting on top of it.

Usually, after they had eaten and while they waited for the kettle to boil, the men dozed a little, pulling at their pipes occasionally and admiring the view of the sunlit sea. Now and then someone would make a remark, which would be answered slowly and drowsily after a long pause. The turf stack was warm from the sun and they would lie like cats against it, at their ease.

Today was quite different. They hardly lay down at all, but kept walking about, pointing downhill and arguing excitedly among themselves. The boys moved nearer to hear what they were saying.

"I don't want to leave my house, God knows," said Jim Connor, "where my people lived always. 'Tis a handy place for going to the sea, and it's at the edge of all my fields. 'Tis a warm house too. 'Twill take twenty years to warm the next house I'll build."

"A new house is terribly cold," the others agreed. "And even when it's warmed up, it doesn't feel right for years and years."

"But I can't afford to lose a sow and fifteen bonavs with every high tide," said Jim Connor. " 'Twill take a year to make up for that."

Mike Fagan said gently:

"We were wanting to tell you about that, Jim. 'Tis a blow to you, as we all know, and we know too that it might be our own turn next time. So there's six of us going to give you a bonav from each, the way things won't be too bad."

Jim's eyes lit up with sudden delight, but he said:

"I couldn't take them from you. 'Twas my own misfortune and I must put up with it."

"It might be our turn next," said Roddy Hernon. "We were in luck, not to have our pigs too near the house. That's why we can spare one each. Next year, one of these will have a litter and you'll be set up again."

"I'm heartily thankful to you," said Jim. "I couldn't sleep at night for thinking of those pigs. And Mary was worse. She cared them like she cares the children, always watching them, always running to see were they safe and well. That's why we had them so near the house, so that she could have her eye on them all day. She's tormented since they're gone. She has no one to eat the potato skins, no one to boil yellow meal for." He drew a long, sighing breath. "The day will come when I'll be able to do a good turn for you."

Mrs. Connor was not at the bog that day. It was easy to see that he was longing to get home and tell her the good news, but he had to content himself with going around and shaking hands with every one of his benefactors. Then they went on with the business of deciding where he would build his new house.

So as not to use a piece of one of his precious fields, he wanted to build it either at a place on the bog road where there was a little hard patch of ground, or else in the well field. No one knew who owned the well field now. It had once belonged to a family called Martin, but the last of them had gone to America in the bad times, when there were famines in Ireland, and they had not been heard of since. The ruins of their house still stood in one corner of the field. Brambles and ferns grew everywhere, except on the little path that led to the well. It was a good well of shining, bubbling water and was used by all the families on the south side of the island. But no one had ever wanted to rebuild the house, though its stone walls were still standing. It would have taken very little work to have made a fine house of it again.

"But what would I do if the descendant of one of those Martins were to come back and lay claim to their house?"

said Jim Connor. "Wouldn't I look like a thief and a robber? What would I say to them?"

"You could say: 'Let you be going back now to whatever place you came from,' " said Mike, " 'and long ago you should have come over from America if you wanted your house.' "

"And you could say: 'If you don't leave our island quick, we'll pitch you off it head first,' " said Roddy.

"I couldn't talk like that if my children were listening," said Jim. "What would they think of their father?"

"That he was a good, useful, providing kind of a father," said Mike.

But Jim would not agree.

"If I took possession of that house now," he said, "maybe none of you that are my friends would raise his voice against me. But your children might raise their voices against my children when you and I are dead and gone, or maybe even your children's children. It could be the cause of many a cross word between neighbors. I wouldn't like to face God and I the one to have started that."

"It could be true for you," the others said reluctantly. " 'Tis a fine house and a pity to see it going to waste. But maybe you'd never have luck with it."

"In three weeks or four, then, we'll start on the building," said Jim, "when the evenings will be getting long. Mary is at me since the day of the big wave to move out of our own place. When Father Reilly comes over for Mass on Sunday, we'll ask him to come up and bless the ground for the new house."

When they heard this, the boys knew that Jim Connor

was really going to leave the house where his people had lived as long as the island had a history.

"I never heard of anyone doing the like of that," said Pat. "You'd hear of people leaving their home to go to America, or to go to work in Galway or Dublin or some other city, but I never thought anyone would leave their house and build another one in a different place on the island."

He sounded quite shocked. John said:

"It's a sensible thing to do, better than waiting for another wave to come along, in the middle of the night, maybe, when no one would have warning. And you'd best get used to the idea because if they're all going to move away from the sea, we'll have to persuade Sally to move too. You can be thinking of how that's going to be done."

"She'll never move," Pat said positively. "I know her." He gave a sudden short laugh. "And sure, I'm as bad as her. I think it's a terrible thing to go against your forefathers, making yourself different, thinking you can be better than them."

"How do you know what your forefathers would have done if they were alive today?" John demanded. "When they lived, there weren't any big waves like the ones that are there nowadays. Times have changed. I don't believe our forefathers would have sat like rocks waiting to be swallowed up by the sea. And let me tell you that if you don't ask Sally to move, she won't stir. She certainly won't move for me, nor for Tom Faherty, nor for Jim Connor, nor for any of the other people that will be advising her. You must agree with me when I tell her she's got to move if everyone else does."

For the rest of that day, whenever they were near each other John tried to force Pat into understanding the importance of persuading Sally that she would have to move if all her neighbors did. But it was no use. Later in the evening, after he had had his own supper at home, he went down to the quay and found that Pat had not even told Sally what the men were planning.

"And it's very sensible," he said when he had told her himself. "It's nearly as sensible as getting the sea wall rebuilt. At least they will be safe when they're off the low ground where the waves come."

"And how do we know the waves won't come higher and higher? How do we know they won't wash over the whole island some day, and drown every man, woman and child on it?"

"There's no sea wall would keep out a wave like that," said John.

"It's what will happen if the present wall is not mended," said Sally. "Little by little, the lower part of the island will be washed away until the job of protecting Inisharcain from the sea will be so big that no one alive will be able to do it. Then everyone will have to leave the island altogether, even the people like yourself that are now living high and dry and safe."

John felt a sudden sharp pang go through him at this thought. Now he realized that when he had been talking to Pat all day about the necessity of his moving, it had somehow seemed quite certain that his own house was beyond all danger. Sally was saying:

"Once I went to Inisheer, and I saw the remains of

houses, and a whole church buried up to the gables in the sand. That was a terrible sight, and one that never after left my mind. I'm not going to let the same happen in Inisharcain, not if I have to spend the rest of my life working to prevent it."

"What can we do, that we haven't done already?" John asked in despair. "We wrote to the County Council. That's all anyone can do."

"However we do it," said Sally, "we must get engineers out to work on the wall."

"When the engineer came, the men threatened to throw him into the sea."

"We were unlucky. We'll have to try again."

"How?"

"Someone must go in to Galway."

"Will you go?"

"Don't you know well I'll never see Galway again, at my age?" Sally said. "Yourself and Pat will go."

"We'll never get leave."

"There's no one to stop Pat but myself. And it looks as if you'll have to go without leave." She chuckled at his shocked look. "I'll give you leave, if you like. Wasn't my father a second cousin to your great-grandfather? That gives me a right to give you orders."

That did not seem quite right to John, but he put the problem aside for the moment. He could see that Sally had some plan in her mind which she had not yet explained.

"What would we do in Galway?" he asked.

She leaned forward eagerly to tell them.

"You'll go to a meeting of the County Council, where all the wisest and the cleverest men in Connacht will be gathered together in one big room, and you'll tell them all about our sea wall. It will be quite different from writing a letter. There's some things that you can't write in a letter, like that your own neighbors are so ignorant that they would rather risk their lives and the lives of their children than to have strangers working on the island for a few months. That must not be written down because I have heard that in the County Council they don't throw away the letters that they get but they keep them forever and ever."

"Do you mean to say that that letter I wrote about the big wave will be kept forever in Galway?"

"That's what they do. They keep them all in huge boxes so that the people of future times can be going over and over them at their ease."

"You should have told me that before I sent off that letter," John said reproachfully.

He was thinking of how much more care he would have taken with the handwriting if he had known that it would be so long preserved.

If I had told you that, *agrá,* you mightn't have written the letter for me at all," said Sally. "Now you see that we can't write the truth. But if you were at the meeting, the two of you, you could be leaving out little hints about why the people were so cross the day Andy Phelan came. You can say that when the engineer comes, the men of the island could do the work under his eyes. That way we wouldn't have too many strangers about. And you could say, if you got the chance, that I'd keep the engineer here in my house. I have a room in there for him, fit for a king. And then if I saw him inclined to take a ramble up the island of an evening, I'd think of some excuse to keep him at home. I could start up a game of cards, or a dance, and he'd never guess why I was doing it."

"How would we find the place in Galway where they have the meetings?" John asked. "Is it near the docks?"

"No, but you can follow the river up from the docks and you'll come to it. They have their meetings in the Court House. I'll tell you exactly how to get there."

"And how will we know which day to go? Do they have a meeting every day?"

"No, indeed. They're busy people, important people, with a lot of other things to do. But every month, on the first Monday, they leave their own affairs and come in to a meeting, and give their time and their brains to the people of the County."

"They must be very good, unselfish people," said Pat.

"They are that, the most of them, though they don't always get much thanks," said Sally. " 'Tis hard to please everyone. They're good enough that they'll listen to you and do what you ask if they think it's right."

"If you're so sure of that," John said, "we'll go. But won't they think it queer for two boys to be asking for something that's the business of grown men?"

"They'll think it queer, all right, and it will be your business to show them that boys had to interfere when men wouldn't do what they ought. It happens often that way in the world, that the young people have more courage than the grown-up ones."

"What about yourself? You're not young, and you have plenty of courage."

"Young people and old people have courage," said Sally. "That's why they often get on well together. It's the middle-aged people that are afraid."

John almost seemed to feel himself grow bigger at this. The journey into Galway and the visit to the County Council meeting, which a few minutes ago seemed terrifying, now suddenly looked much easier.

"So we'll take a boat and sail into Galway, myself and Pat," he said. "We'd have to leave on the Sunday, the day before the meeting, to be sure to be in time. But it would be hard to get a boat out on a Sunday without being seen, unless we left it until after dark and sailed all night—"

"Glory be to God!" said Sally with respect. "You have courage, indeed." She chuckled. "But I wasn't thinking of sending the two of you off alone in a boat to sail to Galway. There's many a man would be afraid to undertake that journey alone. And anyway, the first thing that would happen is that the boat would be missed and the men would go out after you. Then you'd never get near the County Council."

"How are we to go, then?"

" 'Tis a hard question, and I've been thinking of it for the last hour and more. You could hide on the steamer when it calls, and come out after a while and buy your tickets when you'd be well away from the island."

"But the steamer would have people from Inisharcain on it, that might be wanting to send us back, or that might be watching us while we'd be in Galway."

"It's true, indeed."

That evening they could think of no plan that would be sure to work. They walked down to the quay to look at the boats. Since the storm, this had become a favorite gathering-place in the evenings. The five men who owned the hookers seemed never to be easy about them now, unless they were looking at them. Christy Moran was working on the new mast for his, while the other men leaned in a row against the quay wall and watched him. Christy had a fine piece of driftwood, the trunk of a larch tree, that you would think had been grown specially to make a hooker's mast. He had it laid out on two big rocks, and for days past he had spent every evening walking up and down beside it, as long as the light lasted, planing it and whittling it and polishing it, with an anxious frown forever on his forehead.

This evening he looked more cheerful. Instead of planing and whittling, he was running his hands all over the mast when the boys arrived.

" 'Twill be ready," they heard him say. "Tomorrow I'll step it. I'll be wanting a bit of help. 'Tis a fine heavy mast."

" 'Twill be ready for sure," said the men. "We'll all come down tomorrow night and we'll lend a hand each, or maybe two."

"Ready for what?" John asked innocently, though he had guessed what they were thinking of.

"The May Fair in Galway, of course, on Saturday week," said Stephen Cooney. "The boys these times do be half asleep. When I was young we used to know the day and date of every fair in Galway from Christmas out. 'Twas all written, for them that could read, in Old Moore's Almanac. It used to come out from Galway with the mottoes and the Christmas decorations—"

"It does the same now," said Mike Fagan. "Well you'd know it, if you had a wife and family. Man, dear, you should hear the plans that do be made every Christmas! There's some that think there aren't half enough fairs in Galway."

"I wasn't at one yet this year," said John. "I'd love to go to the May Fair."

It was everyone's favorite fair of the whole year. It was for horses only, and all the people at it were in good humor because they always got good prices there. The weather was usually warm and sunny, with the feel and promise of summer. Horses are such clean, clever animals that it was an unending pleasure to look at them. John and Pat always wanted to go, but so did everyone else. When space was scarce in the boats, there was not much chance of room being made for boys.

"You'd need to build your own hooker, I'm thinking,"

said Roddy Hernon to John's father, Peter. "Your son is needing to go to the horse fair."

"A man doesn't need a boat of his own when he has good neighbors," said Peter quietly.

From this John knew that if he owned a hooker, his father would willingly bring him to the fair. But since he did not, there was nothing to be done. His father could ask one of his neighbors for room in a boat for himself, if he wanted to buy a horse and have it sent out from Galway on the steamer. But for such an important fair, to ask for a place for John would be out of the question.

"What day will you be sailing to Galway?" John asked Christy Moran, trying not to sound too much interested.

"Friday morning," said Christy, while all the men nodded and murmured agreement. "There will be a high tide at nine in the morning, with God's help. It couldn't be handier. If we get a fair wind, we'll be in to Galway before darkness falls. I'll have a good chance of trying out my mast." He ran his hand along it lovingly. "But I know already, 'tis the finest mast that ever stood in a boat."

" 'Twill be a good fair this year," said James Donnelly, in his usual slow, deep voice. "There's horses coming from all over Ireland for it, and buyers from all over the world. They say the Spanish army is coming to buy horses in Ireland."

"Maybe they'll get back some of the fine horses they lost here the time of the Great Armada," said old Tom Faherty.

"The prices will be better than ever, I'm told," James Donnelly went on. "Anyone that has a good horse should bring him to this fair and not be holding him over until some smaller one."

"There's some that say the prices do be better at the smaller fairs," said Roddy Hernon.

"It won't be like that this time," said James Donnelly. "This will be one of the great fairs."

No one asked James why he was so sure that it would be a good fair. Because he had the shop, they knew, he often talked with the business people in Galway. Somehow these people always knew when the good or the bad times were coming and they stocked their shops accordingly. In this way they made sure never to lose their money. No matter how bad things were with the people who lived off the land, the shopkeepers never seemed to look hungry. No one envied them their prosperity, however. They all knew the proverb that a yard of counter is better than twenty-five acres of land, but not a man there would have given up his freedom to stand behind a counter, even if it were stacked with gold.

When the light was quite gone, one of the men said:

"A pint of black porter, now, with a white head on it, and I wouldn't call the queen my aunt."

As they stood up, John noticed that James Donnelly had slipped away in the darkness. He said to Pat:

"Did you ever notice that, how James is always the first to leave a gathering like this? He'll be above in the shop now, waiting for the men when they go up."

"That's how fortunes are made," said Pat. "We'll go up with them. Maybe they'll talk a bit more about the fair. If there was never a County Council meeting, I'd give an eye to go to that fair."

"Did you notice the day of it? It's the second last day of May. That means that the Monday after, there will be a meeting of the County Council."

"The first day of June. Will that count as the first Monday?"

"Of course it will. It would be a great thing if we could get to that meeting. There would be the long summer before us, for mending the wall."

"And we'd see the horse fair as well," said Pat.

Silently they walked up the quay road, behind the men. Sure enough, when they reached the shop, there was James Donnelly already standing behind his long counter. Within a few minutes, every man had a huge glass in his hand, except for Stephen Cooney. As he never worked outside, he had an appetite only for a small one. Perhaps this was why he said to James after a while:

"A bottle of lemonade, James, between the two boys."

They thanked him for his kindness, glad to be given anything at all, and took their two half-glasses away to the end of the counter where they would not be in anyone's way.

Donnelly's was a beautiful shop. It was very long, and the polished counter ran the whole length of it except for a place at the end where you could go in and out. Behind the end nearest to the door, there were barrels of beer and porter on the floor. On the shelves above them, there were bottles of port which would only be used if there were a funeral. Then every woman who came to the funeral would have a little glass of it. As there were not many funerals, the port in Donnelly's lasted a very long time.

The other end of the shop was by far the more interest-

ing. Down on the floor were the sacks which Mrs. Donnelly had prudently stored under the roof at the time of the flood. In the daytime their necks stood always folded back, so that a stone or a half-stone of flour or meal could be shoveled at once into a paper bag for a customer. At this time of the evening the sacks were closed, and Donnelly's old tom cat paced up and down beside them, like a policeman, in case any mouse might think of helping himself in the dimness.

On shelves above the sacks, there were pots of jam and jars of bread-soda and currants, and everything that one could possibly use in a kitchen. Hanging from the ceiling were headstalls and bridles and reins and bits and straddles, as well as ropes that could be used either on boats or for tying a stack of corn. Pots and buckets and pans and oil-lamps hung from the ceiling too, and in among them the two big oil-lamps that lit up the shop, with their soft light glowing through white glass globes. Indeed it seemed that without the things that were in that shop, all work on the island must come to an end.

At the same moment that this thought occurred to John, Stephen Cooney leaned forward and said to James:

"I suppose you'll be the next that will be thinking of changing your house."

"I suppose so," said James, and he looked very uneasy.

Mrs. Donnelly came quickly up from the other end of the shop, where she had been writing figures in a little book.

"Changing our house? Who is changing their house?"

"Jim, here, for one, and I suppose Christy will follow him, and the Hernons. Am I right, Roddy?"

"I'll be thinking of it, I suppose," said Roddy uncomfortably.

Suddenly Mrs. Donnelly threw her blue-checked apron up over her face and burst into howls. The men looked shocked, but no one said a word. She stopped as suddenly as she had begun and glared at them all fiercely.

"Because of the big tide, is it?"

"Yes," said Jim Connor. "We don't know when another one might come. 'Tis better not to live too near the quay in the future, if waves like that one are going to be coming every now and then."

"And will we have to move our shop, that my people had since my great-grandmother's time?"

"Sure, what can we do?" said James. "This time we got the bags and the bottles and the boxes up under the roof. Next time we mightn't be so lucky."

"And how did we get them into safety?" Mrs. Donnelly demanded. "By listening to Sally MacDonagh. And if everyone here present would listen to her now, we'd have our sea wall mended and no one among us would have to insult his ancestors by moving off to a strange place."

" 'Tis true," said Stephen Cooney. "Sally is talking sense about the sea wall. 'Twill have to be repaired."

"Look here, tailor," said Roddy Hernon, " 'tis easily seen you have an innocent occupation. It's a nice thing for you, but we're not all so lucky."

"What could be more innocent than farming the land?" said the tailor.

"There's things about farming that are better kept quiet," said Mike, "things that are a man's private business. And how do we know we wouldn't have a load of taxes put on us, to pay for that wall after? Maybe our children and our children's children would be paying for that wall in the long years that are to come, and it's not praying for us they'd be, for putting a load of debt on them."

"Isn't it better to pay out a little now, than to lose the land under the sea?" said Mrs. Donnelly. "For if the houses go, the land will go with them."

But the men made no answer. She tried again to get them to discuss the question but they just drank their porter and shut their mouths tightly and turned their eyes on the floor, and not another word for or against the mending of the wall could she get out of them. The tailor would not speak either, though she appealed to him several times. But he just sat there, smiling and blinking and pulling at his pipe. As John said, when they were on their way home, the tailor would not go against the men in anything, for fear they would start buying their suits in Galway instead of coming to him to have them made.

"But look how Mrs. Donnelly spoke out, though she has the shop and you'd think she'd be afraid of offending the people."

"Maybe she has courage because we have but the one shop on the island," said John.

"We have but one tailor," Pat pointed out.

" 'Tis true. But you could bring a suit from Galway that would last you ten years, and you must go to the shop every second or third day for something, or die of starvation. It's easier to do without a tailor than without a shop."

"I wonder would Mrs. Donnelly and the tailor stand up for us, if we needed it, if we get the Council to send their engineer again?"

"Mrs. Donnelly would," said John, "and James too, I thing. I don't know what the tailor would do. We'll have to wait and see."

At first it seemed quite impossible that John and Pat would get to the fair. They had never before thought very much about the drawbacks of living on an island away out in the Atlantic Ocean. Now suddenly it felt like a prison, as if the miles of sea that separated it from the mainland were high, unscalable walls. The sea looked rougher, even on a day that they would once have called calm, because now they were constantly thinking of ways of crossing it.

"We could take Sally's currach over to Carraroe," Pat

suggested. "It's only twelve miles. It could be done if we had a good day."

John made no reply except to look out at the dark-blue sea, where little white-topped waves showed their teeth hungrily.

"Sally would never let us go that way, I suppose," said Pat after a moment.

They thought of stowing away in a visiting Connemara hooker, but this would be nearly impossible. There are not many places where you can hide on a small boat. Besides, there was no love lost between the islanders and the Connemara men, and the boys did not feel inclined to trust themselves to their charity now.

Then their opportunity came, so neatly that it certainly seemed, as Sally said, that her prayers that they might get to Galway had been answered.

It began with Pat. He was really sorry for Mrs. Connor. She was one of those women that seem to get every trouble on them—and the troubles that do not come naturally, they bring on themselves. She had five sons, and there was always one of them falling off a wall and cutting himself, or mitching from school, or throwing stones at the neighbors' hens and starting up feuds that might go on forever, or taking out a currach illegally and losing the oars, having to be rescued howling and dripping by half the population of the island.

When each of these things happened, Mary Connor used to be shriveled up with shame for her terrible children, but instead of cuffing them, shouting at them, putting them to work in the potato garden or doing any of the things that the other women would have done, she always received the sinner home like a hero, and cried over him and said he really meant no harm and that you couldn't expect sense from such a young head.

The result of this was that she had the most useless, shiftless family on the island. They never stayed at home, if they could sit on some neighbor's hob and listen to the chat and eat slices of bread and jam. All the people were sorry for them, but, as Sally said, it would have been much better to have chased them home to their mother. Though the eldest boy was eleven, he never helped with the spring-cleaning, nor with any of the dozen things that must be done around a house. Even the smallest one, only four years old, made off every morning at a trot, never saying where he was going and only appearing at home for meals.

Knowing this, Pat had long ago made a habit of going in to see Mrs. Connor whenever he was passing by. Though the Connors were near neighbors of his, still their house was not in the way of being visited because to reach it you had to go up a little laneway. It was true that Mrs. Fagan lived next door, but she was one of those women that are always too busy for a gossip. In this way, it seemed to Pat that Mrs. Connor was often lonely.

He went in as usual one afternoon and found her in a state of despair. The house was tidy enough and there was a fine turf fire, but now he saw with astonishment that the walls inside and outside, and the doors and windows, were untouched by whitewash or paint since the flood.

"You know I was waiting all the time for Jim to get started on it," she said, "but now this morning he says it's not worth while to whitewash this year because we'll be going to the new house. He's up there every minute he can spare, measuring and planning. And sure I know by the way he's talking that it will take the best part of a year, and am I to live in the darkness all that time?"

Afraid that she was going to cry, Pat said:

"I'll do the whitewashing for you. Myself and John made a good job of Tom Faherty's, as he'll tell you, so you needn't be afraid to let us go at it."

Instantly she looked cheerful.

"I heard you did make a fine job of it. And a fine man you're going to be. 'Tis a terrible thing that your own father can't see you reared."

Again she was on the verge of crying for Pat's father, who had been lost at sea twelve years before when Pat was only a baby. He said quickly, almost babbling in his hurry to change the direction of her thoughts:

"We'll do the whitewashing first and the painting after. Have you got paint and whitewash in the house?"

"Not a drop. Didn't I use them all up just before the wave came that drowned my little pigs and turned my house into a bothán? If I had paint and whitewash, I wouldn't have to be asking Jim to do the work for me."

"I'll bring the whitewash," Pat said firmly. "We have a fine lot of lime left over from our own house, and we have paint too."

"The blessings of God on you," said Mary quickly. "I'll make a cup of tea now for the two of us, and we can be talking and planning."

She hung her black kettle over the fire and started getting out soda-bread and butter. A strange thing about her was that she made fine soda-bread, soft and with a taste on it that would be with you all day. Her butter, too, was firm and salty. She loved making these things, and Pat knew that she had told Sally once how she longed to have a daughter to whom she could have passed on her own skills.

Over the tea she said:

"And while you're doing the whitewashing, you may as well mend the hen-house for me. I asked Jim to do it and he made the same answer, that we'll be having a new hen-house at the new house, and it isn't worth while, but sure, we'll have ne'er a hen to bring with us with the way things are going. There's a hole in the side of the hen-house now, that you'd think was made to let in a fox."

"Did the fox get any of your hens?"

"You know the wave got the most of my hens, the way it did with everyone else's, and I'm hatching two clutches of eggs now, so there isn't much for the fox to get. But I can't sleep at night for thinking of my sitting hens, and the little chickens, when they come out, will be there waiting for that red blackguard."

"All right, I'll mend the hen-house too," said Pat. "That must be done."

"And while you're at it, you might as well do the roof of the cart-house. Jim said it wasn't worth while, with the summer coming, but don't we all know we'll get a good share of rain in the summer, and the cart will be rotting away."

By the time he left her, Pat had a long week's work before him. Sally laughed when he told her about it.

"And before I went away, she said I was to be sure to

bring John along as well, because two pairs of hands are better than one."

"What did you say to that?" John demanded.

He was sitting on a low stool by the fire, listening with amusement to the story of Pat's afternoon at Connors', never thinking until now that it had anything to do with him.

"What could I say?" said Pat. "If you don't come and help me out, I'll be working there for a month and I'll get no chance to think of a way of getting in to Galway for the horse fair."

"I'll have to come, of course," John said after a moment. "It's not that I mind the work. Anyone in their right senses would only like to be whitewashing. But it's listening to Mrs. Connor I mind, with her moaning and lamenting. Besides, her own husband and her own sons should be doing those things for her."

"It will be good practice for you, helping out a poor woman that can't do a thing for herself," said Sally calmly. "And I'll tell you something you can remember: the people that need your help are never the good, hardworking, cheerful ones with the children that will do everything for them. They're always the lazy people like Mrs. Connor, that do be grousing and complaining no matter what blessings they have, that spoil their children and drive away their neighbors because they never have a good word for the world. They're a pity, those people, and if they're young and strong like Mrs. Connor, it's all the worse. Now let you go to work for her, and I'll be thinking of a way to get you a spin into Galway on someone's boat, for certain sure."

She was so confident that they felt as if the whole problem were already solved. During the next days, while they worked at Mrs. Connor's after school, they were quite light-hearted. It was a relief to be rid of the nagging fear of something to be done which was quite outside their capacity. But after three or four days in which they pretended to themselves that they had nothing to worry about, suddenly it all came back to them again as sharply as ever.

Mrs. Connor noticed at once that they had become silent and gloomy.

"You're getting tired of working for me," she said in a despairing tone.

"No, no, we're not," they said. "We love whitewashing and painting. We never get enough chances of doing it."

"I can tell by your faces, you're tired of working for me," she insisted, and the well-known whining note came into her voice. "Sure don't I know well how it is with boys, and I having five of my own. They do love to be out playing, and fishing, and talking to the other boys, instead of staying inside helping a poor woman. I do the best I can for you, making tea and all, but there's nothing like being away off with yourselves, free and easy—"

"Listen," Pat said desperately, "it's not because we're tired that we're a bit gloomy today. It's because we hear all the talk of the horse fair next week, the big May Fair where everyone in their senses wants to go. And we have a longing to go to the fair, but we know there won't be room on any of the hookers for us."

"And it isn't because of my whitewashing at all?"

"No. Only because of the fair."

"Thanks be to God," said Mary. "If I thought it was I

was making you down-hearted, I'd die of shame, so I would. And isn't it a terrible thing that the two finest boys on this island, that never see a person in need but that they put out their hand to help them, should be in the want of such a small bit of fun and that they couldn't just ask someone that has a hooker to take them in to Galway—"

By the time that she had said this, the tears were pouring down her face. She lifted the corner of her apron to wipe them away. Pat said in despair:

"What is it to a ship going down? Won't we get there sometime or other?"

She was hardly listening to him. A new thought had struck her.

"And a minute ago, when you said how you wanted to go to the fair, I said: 'Thanks be to God,' thinking only of my own side of the story. And sure, now you'll be insulted—"

And she was in a flood of tears again.

Standing on the kitchen chairs with their whitewash brushes hanging helplessly, the boys looked down at her. They could not decide whether it would be more polite to go on with the work as if nothing were happening, or to try to console her with more words. The trouble was that anything they said seemed likely to produce wails from her. By a lucky chance, just then Sally came strolling into the kitchen. She was knitting a stocking, and she had the ball of wool tucked under her arm so that she could walk about comfortably as she worked.

She understood at once what was happening.

"Now, in the name of all that's wonderful, Mary," she said, "what have you got to cry about? Haven't you your

new house building and your old house being painted, and your husband and your children healthy and strong?"

"It's not for myself I'm crying at all," Mrs. Connor said indignantly, "but for these two poor, hard-working boys that can't have a day's fun and outing."

" 'Twould be more fitting to do something about it," Sally said briskly. "Crying is no good to anyone."

"And what can I do?" She was so much surprised that her voice sounded quite ordinary.

"Hasn't your Jim got a hooker? Can't you make him take the boys in to Galway with him?"

" 'Twill be full up. Every place is booked on it for six months."

"He could make room for a boy. And he could get someone else to make room for another boy."

"He could not."

Mrs. Connor's voice was as hard and cold as a stone now. Watching her from their high perches, the two boys were amazed at the change in her. It almost seemed as if it were a different woman altogether, from the soft helpless creature for whom they had sacrificed so many sunny afternoons. Very slowly, John lifted his eyes to meet Pat's, and he saw that Pat had understood, as he had, what Mrs. Connor was really like. Sally was saying softly:

"Let you take this chance, now, of doing a good turn for another person. If you don't, do you know what the people of Inisharcain might be saying about you?"

"No."

"They might be saying that it's a queer thing how the Connors lost so little by the big wave, after all the howling and wailing they had. They might be noticing how six little pigs came into your pig-house, and two clutches of eggs, and two fine fat hens to sit on them, came into your henhouse. They might say that while every able-bodied woman on the island had to do her own whitewashing twice over, Mary Connor was able to get free labor to do hers. Once they start saying that class of thing, the next could be that the men wouldn't be too quick to give their evenings to building the new house."

She paused. John was shocked at hearing such straight talk. This was the kind of thing, he thought, that should be kept for kitchen gossip. It was uncharitable talk, and only half true besides. Later in the evening, he said some of this to Sally.

"I know 'tis true for you," she said. "But when you're hard pushed, you have to do hard things. I suppose it would do none of us any good to hear the things that are said about us. Mary Connor is lazy, we say, and she'd make the cat work for her, if she could. But maybe she gets tired when another woman wouldn't. People say: 'Why doesn't she put manners on those five rascals of boys she has?' But I think a person's mind is like their body. If you're born with a strong one, you can do wonders and no thanks to you. It's as easy for you as it is for the weak people to do the little they're able for."

"That's what I think," said Pat. "Myself and John will be weak enough, though, by the time we have finished her house for her."

"Won't it be worth it, if she gets you in to Galway?"

They could hardly bear to think of that. They remembered well the narrow-eyed look of Mrs. Connor when

Sally had finished working on her, and the hard tone in which she had said, over and over:

"I'll fix it for them. Just leave it to me and I'll fix it for them."

"I won't exactly leave it to her," Sally said. "I'll be in and out, to see how she's getting along."

Each day when school was over they ran down at once to find out if she had had any news during the morning. When it came at last, however, they were both there to receive it. On his way down to the quay one evening, only two days before the boats would sail, Jim Connor called at Sally's house. He stood inside the door, blocking the light, and he said awkwardly:

"Sally, I heard tell that the young lad wants to go in to Galway to see the horse fair."

"That's right," said Sally casually.

"I'd like to take him on my boat," said Jim. "Mary was telling me—" He paused for a moment and then began again: "I'd like to take him. Mary says he did all the whitewashing and the painting and the mending that was to be done."

"Himself and John together," said Sally quickly.

"Christy Moran will take John, the way they can be having a bit of fun together in Galway. It wouldn't be much good for Pat alone. It's only a small thing I can do until we're on our feet again, but I'd like to do that for them after all the good things that were done for me. I hope you'll let him go, Sally?" he finished anxiously.

"Yes, he can go," said Sally calmly. "Now tell me one thing. What did your Paddy say when he heard you were taking another boy in to the fair and not himself?"

"It's what I said that matters," said Jim. "I told him that the year he'd do the whitewashing, I'd bring him to the fair."

"Good man, yourself," said Sally.

They waited until Jim had gone away from the door before the three of them did a dance around the kitchen. Then Sally sat down on the hob, panting.

"Now we'll start planning what you'll do in Galway," she said, and she added with a chuckle: "I'm afraid I'm a bit old for dancing."

The next day seemed to pass in a dream. School was a torment. They had to sit quietly and force their minds to work on arithmetic and geography when all the time Sally's instructions were steaming and bubbling in their heads. When school was over Pat said:

"I never put down such a day. I wish we could have found some excuse for staying away."

"If we had, everyone would have guessed that there was more to this trip than just going in to look at the horse fair."

"How will we remember all the insrtuctions?" Pat wondered.

"What one will forget, the other will remember," said John. "That's why there must be two of us. Anyway, you may be sure that Sally will give them all to us again."

He was right in this. They had no sooner reached her house than she started on them, how to get to the Court House, likely places where they might sleep, what to say to the County Councillors, how to be sure that a search would not be made for them at the time on Sunday morning when the boats were due to return home. This was her latest idea and the answer had come to her during the night.

"There's only one way to do it, that I can see," she said, "and that is for John to let on he is coming home on Jim Connor's boat for a change and Pat that he will be on Christy Moran's. Each man will think the other is foolish to overload his boat with an extra passenger, but neither of them will want to talk about it for fear the other man might change his mind. Both of them will be glad to be rid of you. I've heard them talking. It's really true that the boats were full before you were added in."

"One thing we didn't talk about," John said suddenly. "How are we going to get home again?"

"With the engineer on the pilot boat."

"You mean that if we don't succeed in getting the engineer to come again, we'll have no way of coming home?"

"That's one thought you can't waste time on," Sally said. "If you're in a tight enough corner, you'll think of something."

"Cold comfort," said Pat, but there was no time to talk any more of this problem.

On Friday morning, the boys were down at the quay at seven o'clock. It was a perfect morning, with the sea shining, silky green, dark-blue towards the horizon. The tide was flowing, and the small, smooth waves rolled in gently onto the strand with a sound no bigger than a whisper. Christy Moran was there already, moving the stones that he had for ballast an inch here and there to improve the balance, going over his ropes and sails. He looked so nervous that the boys were afraid to go near him, though they longed to go over to the edge of the quay and look down at what he was doing. But in a moment Christy called out:

"Let ye come on down here on the boat. Man, isn't it a lovely day? We'll be off at nine o'clock sharp and in at the Claddagh of Galway for sure at nine this evening. A fine day for testing out a boat."

Once they were on board, with the sea shifting under their feet, a great feeling of happiness swept over them. There was no need to talk. They could not sit still, but moved about gently and quietly all the time, now looking over the side at the green floor of the little harbor, now coiling ropes, tidying away cans and nets, trying to keep themselves busy.

At eight o'clock, the other men began to appear. They were very quiet too, while they loaded the bags of wool that they were bringing in to Galway to sell. Their voices came clearly and softly over the still water. The creaking of the blocks as they hauled up sail sounded unnaturally loud in the dry air. Little by little, the early sting went out of the morning, so that the boys began to find their thick jerseys unpleasantly hot. They did not take them off, however, for they knew from experience that once they would be at sea the breeze would cool them down quickly enough.

Shortly before nine o'clock, Pat went ashore to go on Jim Connor's boat. While he was standing on the quay, Sally came hurrying along, swinging a bulging white flour bag firmly tied at the neck with many knots.

"Here is the message, Pat," she said, handing him the bag. "Look after it well."

This was their food for the days when they would be in hiding in Galway. She had a smaller parcel for him too, of food for the journey. John watched Sally's old cat, that had come down to the quay with her, sniff about the big bag which he knew must contain some bacon, as well as loaves of new soda-bread. Pat made a darting movement towards the cat, calling out:

"Get away, you little villain!"

Several of the men looked up uneasily and Stephen Cooney, who was going to Galway to buy cloth, said sharply:

"Don't you know 'tis unlucky to chase a cat away from a boat? Do you want to sink the whole fleet of us?"

"Sssh!" said the men who heard this. "'Tis unlucky to talk of sinking too."

"Catch that cat and pet him," said Stephen, "or I'm going on no boat."

Pat had to call the cat and lift it up in his arms. It rubbed its head against his and purred. Stephen said:

"All right. He's not offended."

Pat held the cat on his shoulder, where it lay comfortably purring, until it was time to go aboard. Watching them,

John thought what a strange thing it was that beating a cat away from a boat should be thought unlucky, whereas giving the same treatment to a boy would seem all right. Cats have the world very well arranged for themselves, he thought: the best place at the fire, the best scraps of food, milk fresh from the cow and the respect of the whole community. It was something to do with their soft movements and round-eyed, unblinking stare. He remembered the story of the three blessings asked by the cat in the old times: soft walking, sight in darkness and forgetful housewives. These last were to leave bits of food where they could be conveniently stolen, but with Sally there was no need for that, she attended so well to her cat's needs.

Just as they cast off, John's mother hurried down the quay road with his parcel of food and some money in a twist of paper.

"Three yards of flowery cloth for an apron," she said, "and a little white tablecloth if they're not too dear. And mind yourself in that big city, not to be run over. And stay quiet in the boat. And tell Kate Fagan I was asking for her. And have a look in the shops in Galway for a nice picture for beside the fire—"

By this time they were at the point of the quay. There was such a calling out of mesages from everyone that he could hardly hear what his mother was saying. He went over her list in his mind so that whatever happened he would be sure at least to please her in these.

It was a wonderful journey. The wind was light but steady. The hookers trailed out across the pale sea, all five of them sailing so fast before the wind that it almost seemed as if they were racing each other. Christy Moran let out a great yell of delight in his good boat and his new mast. Stephen Cooney smiled gently and pulled on his pipe where he lay taking the sun on a bag of wool in the bows.

"Strike up 'The Queen of Connemara' for us, Christy," he said.

But Christy would not. He was shy of boasting of his hooker though he was very pleased at this compliment to her. One of the other men sang it instead:

"Oh, my boat can safely float
In the teeth of wind and weather
And outrace the fastest hooker
Between Galway and Kinsale.
When the black floor of the ocean
And the white foam rise together,
High she rides in her pride
Like a seagull through the gale."

They all took up the chorus:

"Oh, she's neat, oh, she's sweet,
She's a beauty, every line.
The queen of Connemara
Is that bounding barque of mine."

From away off across the water they could hear the men singing in the next boat too.

Soon they were passing by the Aran Islands. A few hookers were putting out to sea and the men gazed across eagerly, hoping to recognize them. Many of the Aran people went to the Galway fairs on the steamer which called twice a week, but there were still a few who preferred to be independent.

After that, they were inside the shelter of Galway Bay, with the long range of the Clare mountains on their right. The mountains were a heavenly pale blue today, with patches of white rock showing here and there and sometimes the little white houses of a village. As they came nearer to Galway, more and more black-painted, black-sailed hookers put out to sea from the Connemara coast, so that by evening, John thought, it looked as if Galway were going to be invaded by a fleet of pirates.

At Galway, the Inisharcain boats were always moored at the Claddagh Dock. It was a difficult mooring to reach because the rushing mouth of the Corrib River had to be crossed at exactly the right point. It seemed as if every man in the boat thought John had secret intentions of wrecking it, they shouted at him so fiercely to keep still. Since he had been sitting motionless on Stephen Cooney's woolsack for more than an hour, this did not seem reasonable. He supposed that they always shouted at the youngest person there, and he wondered which of the men would have been the victim if he had not been present.

The river was safely crossed and the hooker sailed in on the black, oily water of the little dock. They had made good time, the men said with satisfaction. It was eight o'clock, as they could see by the great clock on top of Saint Nicholas' Cathedral. The tide was almost full again, so that they were able to moor comfortably by the steps.

Stephen Cooney climbed stiffly ashore, looking relieved. He never enjoyed these trips to Galway, which he made only twice in the year. He had a sister who was married and lived by the fish market, at the other side of the docks. He always stayed at her house, and now after a word to the men he set off to walk there. Jim Connor said apologetically to John:

"I promised your mother that we wouldn't leave you sleep on the boat. You're to sleep above at Kate Fagan's, where the women always go."

With a burst of rage John remembered how confident his mother had been that he would see Kate Fagan. Jim was watching him uneasily, knowing that he would be angry at not being allowed to stay with the men.

"Pat is to go to Kate's place too," Jim said softly. "With the two of you together, there's no fear you'll be smothered by all them women."

This was good news. John began to see that there were advantages in being at Kate's. If they were to sleep on the boats, either of the owners might decide to sail early on Sunday morning and there would be less possibility of escape.

"I'll like it fine at Kate Fagan's place," he said. "Long enough I'll be sleeping on boats, I suppose."

He climbed ashore. Pat was already waiting for him, swinging the bag of provisions by the neck and glowering with fury at the idea of going to the women's lodging. But as they walked up to the canal bridge, John pointed out that this arrangement would leave them much more free. No women had come from Inisharcain this time, and the few that they could see, who had come on the Connemara boats, looked all taken up with their own affairs.

"When we leave Kate's place on Sunday morning, we can go where we like," John said. "And we may as well sleep comfortably these two nights because maybe we won't sleep at all the nights after that. And there's one thing certain, she'll feed us well. I'm so hungry this moment, I could eat herself, if she's not careful."

There was no need for this. Kate Fagan had a thatched house, just like an island house, in a little square at the western side of the town. She was an Inisharcain woman who had emigrated with her husband to Galway. She loved the fair days and the market days that brought all her friends in to visit her, and she could not conceal her disappointment at having only two boys this time.

"There was no room in the boats, except for the men," John explained. "There were no women at all came this time. We were lucky to get our chance."

They told her a little of how they had managed to get this great privilege, but of course they said nothing of why they had wanted it so badly. She had prepared enough food for six, not knowing how many women would come. Now she placed a huge meal in front of them, of bacon and cabbage and potatoes, and watched anxiously while they ate, urging them on if they seemed to be going more slowly.

"And afterwards you can take a walk down the town," she said. "And when you come back you can tell me everything you saw. There's great doings in Galway this evening, I'm told."

"Couldn't you come with us?" Pat said, for she had a longing note in her voice.

But at that moment the door burst open and in marched an army of four huge Connemara women, made even more immense by their pale brown shawls which covered their baskets of eggs, so that they stuck out oddly at one side.

The oldest one called out, as if she were calling her husband home from three fields away:

"Kate Fagan, we heard you have no island women with you and that maybe you'd have a place for us."

She welcomed them immediately, of course, and set about getting them a meal. The boys slipped outside.

"It's well we got there before them," Pat said. "Any one of that four could have eaten the whole dinner, by the looks of them."

Galway was crammed with people who had come in for the fair. On such a fine evening, they were able fully to enjoy each other's company. They crowded the foot-paths and spilled out onto the road and filled the shops where food and black porter could be bought. Horses were tethered everywhere, in all the narrow side streets and in every possible yard and stable, so that the air quivered with their whinnying. The real selling would not start until the morning, but already little groups of three or four men were to be seen huddled over clenched fists, which showed that bargains were being made.

Up at the square, the tinkers had set up stalls for selling sweets and oranges and lemonade. They were doing very little business this evening and they had left the stalls in charge of the children while they went looking for their friends. Several of the children had accordians and they were passing the evening usefully in playing on these, stopping to collect pennies in their caps from time to time. One boy was able to play waltzes. A crowd gathered around him as the evening went on, and then some of the people began to dance. John and Pat stayed to watch. It was nearly night. The swallows swooped and shrieked above them, so high that they looked like flies against the darkening sky. The last of the sunlight caught their flashing wings as they turned. Then the lamplight seemed to get stronger. Suddenly they both felt heavily tired.

They left the square and walked down through the narrow main street of the town, crossed the bridge over the tumbling, rolling river and came at last to Kate's house.

It was much darker in this part of the town and there was an eerie feel about it, perhaps because of the wide open doorways which were full of people that they could not see, though they could hear them talking softly and laughing in the darkness. Everywhere there were horses. Their hooves rang on the cobbles when they shifted their feet, their headstalls rattled when they shook their heads, and occasionally there was a soft whinny.

The boys pushed open the half-door of Kate's kitchen and went inside. It was like walking into an oven. On either hob, still wearing their shawls, two of the Connemara women sat. Directly in front of the fire, and huddled over it, sat the other two. Well away from the fire, Kate was standing at the table making a soda-loaf. The four women were not interested in her. They were exchanging gossip and jokes at the tops of their voices, swaying up and down with laughter so that one wondered they were not afraid of falling into the fire.

Kate was clearly glad to see the boys come in. She made a huge pot of tea and within a few minutes they were eating again. Then they had to tell her how things were with everyone on the island. The four Connemara women were silent now, listening eagerly for a good story to bring home from the fair. Seeing this, the boys were very careful in their account of doings on Inisharcain. In fact, by the time they had finished it seemed as if that island were a heaven of peace and comfort and prosperity, where neighbors vied at doing good turns for each other, where the animals and the children and the crops were so healthy that no one ever lost a night's sleep over them.

There were tears of homesickness in Kate's eyes as she showed the boys to their beds in a tiny room off the kitchen. In the light of the candle they looked at each other and chuckled. Then they leaped into bed, and without a single word in five minutes they were asleep.

The clanking of donkey-carts woke them in the morning. An endless procession of them was passing by the side of the square, loaded with vegetables and kegs of buttermilk and boxes of butter and eggs. Some of the carts had high sides and carried little pigs or calves. They were coming from the country, as much as seven or eight miles outside Galway, and they had been on the road for hours, they moved so slowly. Now and then, one would turn aside into the little square in front of Kate's house. There the donkeys were unharnessed, the carts tilted back on their tails, and sacks of potatoes displayed for sale.

Only potatoes were sold in that market. The boys watched them for a while but they were not very interesting, being all the same. When they had eaten, they walked up to Saint Nicholas' Cathedral. Behind it was the main market. Here the carts of vegetables had come to rest, and their contents were being sold briskly to the people of the town. There were other wonderful things there, cups and plates, pictures and statues and lamps, pots and kettles and pans. They could have stayed all day just in that market, but soon John pulled Pat away.

"This market is here every Saturday," he said, "but the May Fair comes only once a year. Come and look at the horses."

All the way up to the square, they had to push their way through the crowds of people who seemed to be moving as slowly as possible. The men, in their wide-skirted black Sunday coats, stepped deliberately, holding their ash-sticks clutched in their clasped hands behind them. The sticks stuck out like tails, and more than once, in their hurry, the boys got them between their shins and almost fell over them. The women seemed all to be as wide as the four that had lodged at Kate Fagan's. Tired of carrying their heavy baskets, when they stopped to gossip they laid them on the ground between their feet, ready to catch at the toes of anyone in a hurry.

At last the boys reached the square. It was a wonderful sight. Never had they seen such horses. They were all sizes, some so tall that their owners had to stretch away upwards to catch at their bridles. These were mostly hunters, good for jumping, slim and clean and elegant, with delicate mouths and well-brushed tails and manes. There were cobs and ponies, good for riding too, but not above pulling a trap or even a cart. There were the powerful Irish draught horses, that looked so slight but could do as much as three of any other breed. There were a few huge shire horses as well, with hooves as big as dinner-plates, and great, slow, velvety eyes, and sides and haunches like elephants. And everywhere there were foals, with pointed ears and wild round eyes that seemed to look in every direction at once, and tails that still had not hair but only fur. They pranced and danced on their little feet, but they kept so close to their mothers as to be always just touching them.

John made a decision that day.

"When I grow up and have my own land," he said, "I'll breed horses. I'll have nothing but horses."

All day they walked in a kind of dream among the horses, stopping now and then to listen to bargains being made. Prices were high, as James Donnelly had said they would be, and all the people who had horses to sell were in good humor. The buyers seemed to be in good humor too, but it was harder to tell with them because they always had a false, hearty way of talking so that there was no way of knowing what they were really thinking. While they talked to the owners of the horses, they seemed to be their closest friends. A moment after they had turned away, you could see that they had forgotten them.

The best horses were bought by well-dressed, fast-moving men with hard eyes, who ran their hands over the horses' flanks as if they intended to ride them themselves. The owners of the horses knew well that these were always

hoping to pick up a champion show jumper or a first-class race horse for a few pounds, to boast of for the rest of their lives. These men came from Limerick or Kildare or Dublin, where the big stud farms were. Sometimes they had brought horses with them, to sell to each other. When this happened, they never made their bargains in the natural way, spitting on the ground, banging the fist of buyer and seller together, and ending up with a drink paid for by the seller. Instead they stood quietly side by side, muttering to each other out of the corner of their mouths.

"Look at them!" said Jim Connor, whom the boys met in the square, watching a pair of buyers discussing the price of a fine hunter that a groom was holding before them. "Look at them! 'Tisn't Christian. I hope I'll never see the day when we'll all be doing our business like that."

Two tall, dark-skinned men were there, buying horses for the Spanish army as had also been foretold by James Donnelly. Jim Connor pointed these out, as well as a pair from Vienna who were looking for show jumpers.

"And they know where to come for them," said Jim. He

was leading a little red pony that he had bought in the morning. He kept on saying: "Isn't he a beauty? I got him first thing this morning, a great bargain. I wish I could bring him home on the boat with me, but 'twould be too dangerous. I'll have to send him on the steamer. Isn't he a beauty?"

As the day went on, gradually the horses were fewer and fewer. The best of the work-horses had been bought by those heavy-looking, slow men who never took their hands out of their pockets, whose overcoats were always swinging open and who all had a way of rolling up and down on their feet from head to toe, to help them to think. When these had got what they wanted, the tinkers who were horse-copers bought the rest. Even they gave good prices on that day. The boys saw them going about with strings of eight or ten horses, pulling them through the crowds of people without even turning their heads to listen to the abuse that was being shouted after them.

It was a day to remember forever. The sunshine, the dust, the smell of horses, the shuffling crowds, the bright stalls, the excited faces of the people and the music of ballad-singers and accordians and fiddles, all together made them feel as if they had lived through three days instead of one. Inisharcain seemed a thousand miles away. Even the Galway County Council did not now seem such a terribly important institution as it had yesterday. Neither of them had spoken of the business that had brought them to Galway. It seemed that there was no need, as if an agreement existed between them not to mention it on this wonderful day. And yet both of them knew that if you enjoy your reward in advance of the work done, this seems to be an extra reason why you must succeed in it when the time comes.

Perhaps this was why, when they woke the next morning, they had no thought of having another day's fun. There was so much to do, and especially so much careful thinking, that they had no room in their heads even for remembering yesterday. One mistake this morning and they would be swept back to Inisharcain without having any chance of doing what they had come for.

It was strangely quiet. Not a cart, not a hoofbeat could be heard. The little square outside Kate's door drowsed in the Sunday sun, so that one could hardly imagine it was the same place that had so hummed with life the day before. As they walked to the Claddagh church they saw that not only the shops but also the house doors were closed up tightly, as if the people inside felt that they had had enough company to do them for a long time.

At the Claddagh they saw that one or two hookers were already at sea. John felt his chest squeeze in and out with fright. The Inisharcain men were on their way into the church in a group. Jim Connor called out when he saw the boys coming:

"In good time, my passenger!"

"And mine," said Christy Moran.

Suddenly John saw clearly what he would have to do. Ever since they had left Inisharcain quay he had been thinking of how to stay behind in Galway when the boats sailed. Sally's solution had seemed easy enough at the time that she suggested it, but now he found that he could not bring himself to use it, especially on the very threshold of the church. He pulled Jim's jersey sleeve until he had got his attention. Then he said in a low voice:

"Jim, I'm thinking you were never told we won't be on the boat back with you."

Jim started and his eyes narrowed.

"Not on the boat going back? Why?"

"It's a message we have to do for Sally tomorrow, myself and Pat."

"What message?"

"It's a private message," John said desperately. "She doesn't want anyone to know about it. But she knows we have to stay over."

He saw Jim glance quickly towards his hooker and guessed what was in his mind, that if he had one passenger less he would be able to take on some extra cargo. A boy takes up as much room as a sack of meal and is far less useful. Still he asked again:

"Sally knows you're staying?"

"Yes."

"It's a wonder she didn't say it," said Jim. "I bet it has something to do with a pension. And sure we'll all be getting odd when we'll be getting old. Are you nice and comfortable above in Kate Fagan's?"

"Fine."

"Good, good. I'll tell Christy that you won't be with him."

And that was his last word. It almost seemed, indeed, as if he moved away from John quickly, in case he might hear something that would make him change his mind about leaving him behind.

Before they went into the church, John told Pat what he had done.

"It was a risk," said Pat. "Now we'd best keep a mile away from him for fear he'd start asking questions."

But there was no need. When they came out of the church, Jim did not even glance in their direction. When they saw him go towards Christy Moran, they walked away slowly, wishing that instead of the wide spaces around the docks there were narrow streets where they could run and be lost at once. But they had to seem to be in no hurry, to be interested in looking at the river, and the Claddagh hookers, and especially at the little fleet of Spanish trawlers that was moored in the next dock. Fortunately, these were taking the attention of all the Inisharcain men. No one called after the boys to tell them that they were going in the wrong direction, to say that this was no time for rambling off and to ask if they wanted the whole expedition held up for their worships alone.

At last they had crossed the Wolfe Tone bridge and were in the fish market. Now they were far enough away to feel safe, and still they were able to see the hookers clearly at the other side of the docks. Leaning against the sunny wall of the Spanish Arch, they watched the men haul up sail and put to sea. One by one, the hookers began to dip before the slow waves. Then their black hulls seemed to disappear, and at last there were only the tall black sails like specks on the huge, grey-blue sea.

"They'll be a long time going home," said John after a while.

"All day," said Pat. "We'll have time for everything."

They knew that dressed as they were in the island

tweed, they would be recognized at once if John's parents were to telegraph to the Civic Guards in Galway about them. Sally had guaranteed not to allow this to happen, but they could not be sure that she would succeed. A good hiding-place had to be found.

"Somewhere about here would be fine," said Pat. "It feels homelike, near the sea and with the smell of fish and the seaweed."

But John said:

"It would be the first place that people would search. I'd feel safer somewhere else."

They noticed that a few old men, who had come rambling out of the houses nearby to sit in the sun, were watching them curiously. Another minute and one of them would start up a conversation. If that happened, they would be remembered forever.

"We'll find the Court House first," said Pat. "Then we'll find a hiding-place near it."

Sally had told them exactly how to reach the Court House, but it took them a long time to find it. All through the town they went, while the sack with their food seemed to become heavier and heavier. The streets had not yet been cleaned after the fair, and they were littered with papers and the peels of oranges and bananas. These gave off a sweet scent in the sun. A few tinkers were still at the square, taking down their tented stall and packing their stock of sweets and fruit and lemonade bottles into boxes.

"I wonder where did they sleep last night?" said Pat.

At that moment they saw, when the stall was taken to pieces, that some old blankets had been laid out underneath it, and there the whole family of tinkers had slept.

"If they can do that, so can we," said Pat, "only that we have no blankets."

They stood to watch the tinkers load their property onto a tiny donkey cart and drive off.

"It would be a great life," said John enviously. "A little donkey and cart, and a tent, and you could see the whole length and width of the world."

Quite close to the square, after much searching, they found the Court House. They stood to gaze at it. Wide steps led up to the huge door, a bigger door than either of them had ever seen before. The thought of walking in through that doorway was terrifying. It was shut now, because of its being Sunday, but they could well imagine the gorgeousness of the inside.

Beyond the Court House, where the road ran downhill, they could see water shining.

"The river," said John.

It was pleasant to leave the Court House and run down to the river. At its edge, they stopped, amazed at its beauty. It was not in the least like the sea. It was smooth, though it was full of movement. Rushes grew tall at its edges, and elegant, light boats were moored there, with little wooden landing stages, as clean as tables. Where they stood, heavy chestnut trees shaded the water and turned it green with their reflection. Away off in the distance, a line of white limestone pillars crossed the river, where once there had been a bridge.

Silently they walked along to the edge of the river, passing more landing stages, and motorboats with cabins that looked like little houses.

At the same moment, they stopped and looked at each other.

"If we could sleep on one of those—" said Pat.

But the cabin doors were locked. Also, as soon as they boarded one of the boats a man came out of a nearby house and shouted at them angrily to get off it again.

"They're as precious about their old boats here as they are in the islands," said John. "We'd better give up that idea."

Farther on, they found a little grass-grown pier and moored against it a big boat, four times the size of a hooker. It lay so low in the water that they guessed it was full of cargo waiting to be brought up river to the lake. All of its hatches were firmly closed down and its cabin doors securely locked.

"The people of Galway must be very dishonest," said Pat in disgust, after they had tried every possible means of going below. "Otherwise why would they have to lock up everything so carefully?"

"Maybe they knew we were coming," said John.

At last they found what they wanted, an old stone warehouse facing the pier. It seemed not to be in use at all. They pushed at the rickety door and opened it easily. There was a huge, dim room with a dusty, uneven floor, and high, barred windows that left the corners full of shadows. Because of the trees outside, the shadows moved eerily. They shut the door and walked softly into the room.

Someone else had camped there quite lately, perhaps during the days of the fair. There was an arrangement of old sacks for a bed, and a box for a table, with a few crusts of bread lying on it. John picked these up and said:

"The bread is not quite hard. If there were rats, they would have eaten it. So long as there are no rats—"

"I never liked rats either," said Pat. "And there is a light outside."

He pointed to where a street light hung near one of the barred windows.

"That means we won't need a candle."

"If we lit a candle, someone would surely come to see who is here."

Without knowing it, they were talking in whispers. Already they were feeling the terrors of the long hours of darkness that they would spend in this quiet place.

"We could go back to the sea and swim," Pat said doubtfully.

But the way back to the docks seemed very long. They brushed the box clean with their hands and opened Sally's bag of food. Sure enough, there was bacon as well as two whole loaves of soda-bread, some butter in a cabbage leaf and a horn-handled knife to spread it with, and a whole clutch of hard-boiled eggs.

They had more courage after they had eaten, but as they carefully wrapped up the remainder of the food in the flour bag, Pat said:

"When we have our business finished in Galway, I don't want to leave Inisharcain again as long as I live."

But John was thinking that for him this was the beginning of a new life, in which he would brave the dangers of the world, doing good to everyone wherever he went, and perhaps coming home to Inisharcain in the end to tell Pat all about his adventures.

During the rest of that day, they stayed near the river. They crossed the bridge below the weir and looked down over the parapet at the shallows where hundreds of salmon lay, with the bubbling water continually tickling their backs. Everyone crossing the bridge stopped for a few minutes to stare. Now and then, long snake-like eels wove their way in and out among the salmon, but seemed never to molest them. Below the weir, the river looked more like the one that they knew, the wild, swift river that flowed into the sea by the docks.

Down there, they could see the old Franciscan Abbey and the other bridge, at the flour mill whose huge wheels had once been turned by this same river.

Farther on, they came to the canal, dark and deep and shining. Here there were more houseboats moored, but now they knew better than to board them. Besides, people came now and then and took one out, chugging slowly upriver, leaving a broadening wake. John longed to go with one of these.

"I've heard that there are thirty miles of the lake up there," he said, "with little grassy islands and people living on them. I'd love to see those islands."

But there was no hope of this. They were afraid to show themselves too plainly interested, lest someone might begin to question them.

As evening came on, the bells rang and the people began to walk in little groups to the churches. They followed one group to the Abbey by the river, and stood in the darkness at the back of the church to listen to the singing. Afterwards they went back to the warehouse, opening the door with great caution, lest someone else might have moved in there during the afternoon.

But it was quite empty. Once they had thought of it, however, they had to peg the door securely shut before they lay down on the sacks after supper. It was still daylight outside, as they could see through the barred window. They did not want to wait for darkness before falling asleep, but the floor was hard and the sacks were thin. Long before they slept, the little yellow eye of the street lamp was looking in at them, making the corner shadows huge and terrifying.

When they awoke, it was daylight. John was the first. It was quiet here away from the town, and only faintly the sounds of the traffic reached him. He listened for a while before awakening Pat. Then he shook him gently by the shoulder until he rolled onto his back and lay staring at the dusty ceiling.

"Such dreams as I had," he said. "The worst was that we were put in jail for disturbing the County Council meeting, and had to sleep on sacks on the floor."

"We'll take our breakfast outside," said John. "I've had enough of this place too."

They carried the flour sack, which was now much lighter, along the river bank to the grassy quay where the big cargo boat was moored. While they were eating, four men came walking along from the direction of the town. Without so much as a glance at the boys, they climbed aboard the boat and began to open the cabin doors and the hatches, and generally to make ready to put out on the river. A fat, slow, rolling man seemed to be their captain. Presently he came out of his cabin and crossed the deck, carrying two huge mugs in his hands. He stood by the rail and called out:

"Hi, you boys! Here's tea for you!"

As the boys moved towards him, he said testily:

"Come along, come along! It's not poisoned. Drink it quickly. I want my mugs back."

"Thank you, sir," said John, leaning up and taking the mugs.

"The other boy has no tongue, I suppose," said the man.

"Thank you, sir," said Pat furiously. "I was just going to say it, only you didn't give me time."

"Hot temper!" said the man. "You'll never get anywhere with that. Always count ten before you speak, if you are hot-tempered. What are you two Inisharcain boys doing here at seven o'clock in the morning, eating breakfast out of a flour bag?"

"How do you know we're from Inisharcain?"

"Your clothes, of course. My grandmother was a Folan woman from Inisharcain, and she married a Joyce man from the Joyce country, my grandfather, that built this boat with his own two hands and the twelve hands of his sons."

"Six sons," said John.

"I see you're good at the sums. You didn't tell me what you're doing here."

"Are you going up the lake now, in a few minutes?" John asked as the boat's engines began to hum gently.

"Yes."

"And how long will you be gone?"

"A week or more, by the time we get to all the villages on the lake with our cargo. Young fellow, you'll go far," said the big man. "Every time I ask you a question, you answer with another. This time you just answer: what are you doing here at this hour of the morning?"

"We came in to go to a meeting of the County Council," said John. "Do you know what time of the day they have their meetings?"

"Another question. I do know, as it happens. At eleven o'clock they begin, and they go on until they get hungry.

What are you going to a County Council meeting for? Have you been elected by the people of Inisharcain?"

He gave a big, hooting laugh.

"Can anyone that likes go in to a meeting?"

"There's a place for the public to sit."

"Are we the public?"

"I think so, for all that you're small size. You can go in by the front door, and up the stairs, and there is a door marked 'Public Gallery,' that looks down on the Council Room. My mugs!" he called out suddenly as two of the other men began to cast off the ropes that moored the boat to the quay.

Quickly the boys handed him the mugs. As the boat moved a yard away from the quay, the fat man shouted:

"You never told me why you're going to the meeting. My house is the tall, thin, yellow one, there. Look, look, look! You can go there tonight, to sleep, if you like. It would be better than sleeping on sacks in my old warehouse! Tell my wife I said you can sleep in Joe's bed!"

He burst out laughing again at the surprised look on their faces. As the boat moved away, they could still hear him laughing in great bursts, walking along by the rail and turning every now and then to look back at them.

"That's a man I'd like to meet again," said John after a moment. "A knowledgeable man."

"He knows too much," said Pat. "He must have peeked in at us during the night, or early this morning."

"Or perhaps he came in the afternoon yesterday, after we had arranged the place for sleeping, and then guessed this morning that it was we who had slept there. That laugh of his had a very satisfied sound about it."

"Too satisfied."

"We needn't worry about him," said John. "He's gone for a week, he said, and our business will be all over by the time he comes back. And he gave us some useful information."

It seemed as if the hours until eleven o'clock would never pass. Panic seized them whenever they realized clearly what they were planning to do. All their lives they had been instructed that until you have reached the full size of a man, you take no part whatever in the policies of grown men. Yet here they were, about to tell a group of strangers where their duty lay.

"If we even had voices like men," said John in despair. "We squeak like seagulls."

"You'll have to do all the squeaking," said Pat firmly. "I'll stand beside you, making faces like someone that agrees with you, but I know well that I won't be able to say a single word."

"That's fine for me," said John indignantly. "What will happen if I dry up and can't talk either?"

"If you do, it will be the first time in your life," said Pat. "Didn't I see you entertaining the bishop for an hour when he came for the confirmations last year, and none of the rest of us able to say a word?"

"He was in need of someone to talk to him, the poor man, after the sail over in the hooker on a rough sea. I only wanted to take his mind off the journey back."

"Well, you can have some idea of the same kind for the County Councillors," said Pat. Suddenly he looked horrified. "Supposing there is no meeting today! Supposing it's put off! After all we suffered today and yesterday, and all the planning and all the shivering with fright at the thought of facing them, maybe there won't be anyone there to face!"

This thought kept returning to torment them until half an hour before the meeting was due to begin.

They hid the flour bag, which still contained some soda-bread and four eggs, under a bush by the river bank. Then they went to watch the entrance to the Court House, from the opposite side of the little square in front of it. One by one, the County Councillors began to arrive. There was no mistaking them. They were not all well-dressed, but they all had the same serious look which showed in their wrinkled foreheads and tight mouths. Some were bald, from worrying about the affairs of Galway County, Pat suggested. There were young ones and old ones and middle-aged ones. They saw Andy Phelan, glancing sharply and anxiously about him to see who else was arriving, and then putting on his smile to greet them. The boys shrank back out of sight, in case he would recognize them, but after a moment John said:

"I don't think we need to worry. He is not the sort of man that would remember boys."

As soon as Andy had gone inside, boldly they crossed to the steps, walked up them and went into the great hall. A huge, wide flight of steps faced them. Without pausing for an instant, they walked up the stairs and turned towards the public gallery. There it was, as the captain had said. They had expected at least an armed guard to be at the door, but there was no one at all about. They opened the door and went into the gallery.

Now they found that they could look down on the

room where the County Council had its meetings. It was just like a school, John thought, with a high desk at the top and rows of benches and tables in front. Behind the desk, the coat of arms of Galway was painted on the wall. Though there was no one at all in the public gallery, they were afraid to speak. They went down towards the front and sat on one of the benches.

The Council Room was beginning to fill up. As each member came in, he sat down and arranged some papers on the table in front of him, looking every moment more solemn. By the high desk there was a long table, and now they saw a tall thin man come in by a side door and lay a big bundle of papers on this table.

"It's Mr. Lynch, the engineer that came to Inisharcain," John whispered. "I never thought he would be here."

A busy-looking man came towards the engineer and spoke with him for a few moments. Then he climbed onto the platform where the desk was, picked up a little hammer and banged the desk with it once or twice, exactly as the teacher did with his ruler when school was about to begin. At once the members stopped chatting to each other and sat down in their places.

Several people had come into the public gallery in the last few minutes. Very quietly the boys sat, hoping that no one would take any notice of them. Most of the people who had come to watch the meeting were men, and they went to the front rows so as to be able to see and hear everything as well as possible. Little by little the bench on which the boys sat was filled up, and they were edged more and more to the end of it.

The man at the desk stood up. The members stood facing him, while he said a short prayer in which he asked a blessing on the doings of the Council. Pat and John joined in with all their hearts, until they saw the people nearby looking at them in an odd way.

The man at the desk said:

"I declare the meeting open."

Everyone sat down. The boys leaned forward eagerly to watch what would happen next. Just then, there was a noise at the gallery door and a man in a navy-blue suit came marching down towards them, hissing angrily:

"Outside! Outside this moment! You're too young to be in here."

"We're not too young!"

"It says: 'Public Gallery.' "

"We're the public, like anyone else."

"We can be here if we like."

Very red-faced, the man said:

"We'll talk about it outside. You're creating a disturbance."

It was true that everyone was looking at them. Even below in the Council Room, some of the members were turning their heads to peer up at the gallery. Pat shrank down, embarrassed, but John said loudly:

"We will not go outside. We have a right to be here. There's no law that says we can't be here."

"There is a law," said the man triumphantly. "Adults only at the meetings."

"Come on," said Pat in a low voice, when he heard this.

"I will not," said John still in the same clear, loud voice. "We came all the way in from Inisharcain to be at this

meeting and we're not stirring until we have what we came for."

For all his boldness, he expected that at any moment the man would seize him and Pat and hurl them out into the passageway. He looked all ready to do it, when the man at the desk, who was facing the gallery, called out:

"What is going on up there?"

The man in the blue suit leaned over the gallery railing to say:

"Two boys in the public gallery, sir. They won't leave it. They're from the islands, they say."

This was said in such a contemptuous tone that all at once John was seized with a black rage.

"Yes, we are from the islands, and I never knew before that there was any crime in that. I always heard that we had rights, like everyone on the dry land of County Galway."

"You come outside and I'll give you rights!" said the man in the blue suit furiously.

"Wait a moment," the man at the desk said. "I want to talk to this boy." He looked kindly at John and said: "The island people certainly have rights. They pay rates like everyone else. What was it that you came for?"

"We came to ask the Council to have our sea wall repaired, so that ourselves and our houses won't all be washed away by the next big wave that comes along."

"We heard of this before," said the man. "We had a letter, and we sent out the engineer and Mr. Phelan to examine the situation."

"You did, to give you your due, but Mr. Phelan made everyone cross with the things he said to them, and the people said they'd rather have the waves coming than himself from this out."

There was a chuckle from a few of the members at this. Andy Phelan leaped to his feet, saying roughly:

"Mr. Chairman, this is highly improper. I'm the elected representative of the islanders and it's my business to see to this kind of thing, not a boy that walks in here without by your leave and disturbs the meeting of this Council. I move that he be ejected and we go on with our other business."

He sat down with a thump and then sprang up again to say:

"And the procedure is all wrong. They're not even a deputation. We've got to keep to our own rules."

"As they're our own rules, we can break them sometime," said the Chairman calmly. "It is indeed highly irregular but sometimes one gains a lot by a little irregularity. Is anyone going to second Mr. Phelan's motion that we refuse to listen to this boy, put him outside, send him home to his people with the news that the Galway County Council cares nothing for their problems?" No one spoke, and after a moment the Chairman went on: "Mr. Phelan has said it is his business to look after the islands, but we all know how difficult it is to get all of one's business done, so we won't grudge helping him out. Send those two boys down here, so that we can talk comfortably."

"This way," said the man in the blue suit, with narrowed eyes full of dislike.

When they stood up to go out of the gallery with him, John found that his feet were tingling and his legs shaking with fright, so that he was almost afraid of falling.

There was no going back now, however. They had to follow the man down the great stairs and along a passageway, until they came to a door with the name in letters of gold: Council Room. A moment later they were standing by the Chairman's desk. The members were all sitting forward, with eyes fixed on them. In the gallery, everyone was leaning over the rail. After this, thought John, a day's shark-fishing would seem like a holiday.

"Now, tell us all about the sea wall in Inisharcain," said the Chairman.

For a moment John's tongue refused to move. It just stuck there, like a dead thing. Then he remembered Sally, how she had trusted them so completely to bring about the rebuilding of that wall, and he found that he was able to speak. It was easy once he had made a beginning. When he came to the part where he had to explain that the men on Inisharcain did not like strangers and were prepared to risk their island's safety rather than admit them, the Chairman said:

"Yes, yes. We understand. They are independent people. They have their own ways of doing things."

So John was able to go on, saying that when the time came to repair the wall, it would be important to have the work done by the islanders themselves, supervised by the engineer.

"That will be easy," Mr. Lynch said. "That is the way I always like to work."

Ten minutes later, the boys were outside on the Court House steps, blinking in the strong sunlight. Slowly they walked down the steps, placing their feet carefully so as not to trip. Slowly they turned towards the river and in a kind of a dream went on until they reached the grassy bank. There they stopped. They looked back. The Court House was invisible. Suddenly John gave a long, hooting yell, the island call for great distances. Then he leaped a foot into the air and began to run towards the quay, so fast that it felt like flying. At the quay he threw himself on the cool grass and rolled over and over, and at last he lay on his back with his arms and legs pointing in four different directions. A moment later he realized that Pat was beside him, in the same position.

"We did it," said John. "They're coming. They're coming tomorrow."

They lay there for a long time, thinking over every word that had been said, remembering the faces of the Chairman, and Mr. Lynch, and of Andy Phelan and the other Councillors. Andy had tried to take the credit for the decision in the end and had even offered to come out to Inisharcain on the pilot boat again.

"We'll let bygones be bygones," he said with his big, hard smile. "I always like to do good to the people—"

But John said in a despairing tone:

"Mr. Lynch will be enough. There's no need to put that long journey on Mr. Phelan."

And Mr. Lynch said:

"I'll go alone, if you please, and stay a few days if there is a bed for me."

"In my grandmother's house," said Pat, and his voice came in a croak because these were almost the only words he had spoken for an hour.

So it was arranged that the boys would come to the docks at ten o'clock in the morning, to go out with the pilot boat.

"How would we have got home," Pat wondered, "if things had not worked out so well? Sally said we could come on the pilot boat with the engineer and that is just where we are doing. I hope she has the ground prepared for us, or we might be coming back to Galway again with the same boat."

They found their bag of food, still safely hidden under the bush where they had left it. A family of ants had moved into it and were trotting up and down the bread. They shook them off and settled down to finish it. Presently John said:

"Now we should go to the captain's house, as he said. Whose bed did he say we could have?"

"Joe's bed. But I'd rather go to Kate Fagan's."

"But we know Kate Fagan's. Let's go somewhere new."

"I like places I know better than places I don't know."

"That way you never learn anything. Come along."

And John started towards the yellow house that the captain had pointed out. He looked back once to make sure that Pat was following him, and then he began to run. Today, since the meeting, it had suddenly become much harder to go slowly than fast. Pat ran too, so that they arrived panting at the yellow house. The moment that they reached it, the door flew open and a small, fat, old woman stood there looking at them. After a moment she said:

"Are you just running, or has the boat sunk?"

"Just running," said John. "The captain—is he the captain?"

"You might call him that, though no one does. He just owns the boat."

"He said to come and tell you that we can sleep in Joe's bed. But if you don't want it, we have another place where we can go."

"Of course I want it. Since Joe went away, I have no company."

"Who is Joe?"

"Our son. He's a sailor. Sails the China Sea."

She was just as curious as her husband had been, and now they felt quite free to talk about how they had spent the morning. They went over every moment of it, and as they talked, gradually it began to seem as if the things they described had really happened, instead of being part of a strange dream.

After a big, comfortable dinner, she took them to the shops and helped to buy the things that John's mother had asked for, the flowery cloth for an apron, the little white tablecloth which turned out not to be too dear, and a strange, blue and gold picture of the Madonna with tiny angels fluttering behind her head, that John thought was the most beautiful he had ever seen.

"She'll be pleased with your day's work," said the captain's wife. "Now we can enjoy ourselves."

In the late afternoon, she took them on the river in a little, light, varnished boat that looked like a toy to them after the island boats. They went between the pillars of the broken bridge, and up between rushy banks where coots and waterhens paddled and dived, until they came to an old grey castle, standing reflected in its own little harbor. It had belonged to the Blakes, one of the Twelve Tribes, the great families of Galway that came there in the thirteenth century, she said. No one lived in the castle now, except jackdaws and badgers, because it had been burned out seventy years ago. And she said:

"In a month's time you can come again and we'll all

go on the big boat up the lake, to all the islands with the groceries, and to all the little villages."

John promised to ask his father if he could do this, but he could see by Pat's expression that it would take some time to persuade him to come too. He would get Sally after him, he thought. She would persuade a person to do anything in the world.

Joe's bed was far more comfortable than the sacks on which they had slept the night before. It was in a room at the top of the house, looking out over the river. Instead of the street light peering through the gloom of the dusty warehouse, they had a window full of stars.

In the morning, they were at the docks at nine o'clock. The pilot boat was lying there, with the mate already on board. All around them, the air was alive with smells of seaweed and salt. They felt suddenly at home again, as if they had been a month away from the sea instead of two days.

Mr. Lynch and the pilot came down along the docks together, sharp on ten o'clock. As soon as he saw them, the mate called out:

"Is Andy Phelan coming on this trip to Inisharcain?"

"No," said Mr. Lynch. "Only myself and the boys, here."

"Thanks be to God," said the mate. "This ship is not big enough to hold that man and me. If I had to travel with him again, I'd surely duck him in the tide before we'd reach the islands."

With its powerful engines, the pilot boat cut through the water at treble the speed of a hooker. Wishing it would go more slowly, the boys sat close together in the shelter of the little cabin, and spoke not a word. After a while, Mr. Lynch came over and said:

"Why are you so gloomy? You should both be very pleased with yourselves, going home with such good news."

"The trouble is that our people may not think it's such good news," said John.

And they told Mr. Lynch the whole story, of Sally's fears that the wave would come again, and of their own visit to the County Council meeting without the knowledge of the islanders.

"Maybe they won't let us land at all," said John.

"When the time comes," said Mr. Lynch, "you leave them to me."

This made them feel a little easier, until the blue curve of Inisharcain rose out of the sea. Then they sat in terror, while it came closer and closer, and while it changed color until it was a misty green, and then its real, clear green with all the white walls of the fields crossing and recrossing it like a net. As they approached the quay, they saw that a great, dark mass of men was standing at the tip, waiting for them. Farther down they could see the red petticoats and blue checked aprons of the women.

"I see Sally," said John. "Look there, to the front, far down."

They waved to her once, and saw her lift her hand in answer. A moment later the pilot boat drifted in to the quay, and they were looking up into a crowd of angry faces.

Roddy Hernon said:

"Good day to you, gentlemen. I'm sorry you won't be

stopping long. Just hand up those two boys here to us and you can be on your way at once."

"No," said Mr. Lynch quietly. "I'm coming ashore to examine that sea wall more closely and then to arrange about repairing it."

"You're doing no such a thing," said Mike Fagan. "Let you just turn around now, nice and quietly, and there will be no crossness between us. 'Twould be a terrible thing if we had to scuttle the boat under you."

A voice from the back of the crowd shouted:

"Ay, that's the way. It wouldn't be the first time, either."

This person was hushed by all the people around him, who sounded shocked. Sensing it, Mr. Lynch called out in a high, strong voice:

"Men of Inisharcain, do you want to see another wave come swooping over the island, or do you want me to fix your sea wall for you, and put you out of danger?"

"We want no foreigners on this island."

"The wave is come and gone. We don't need our sea wall mended."

" 'Tis all a trick to get ashore and start poking and prying into everything."

But James Donnelly spoke quietly above this confused growling:

"If you were to mend the wall, engineer, would you say no more waves will come?"

"From what I saw of it the last time I was here, I'd say we will be able to fix it so that when the waves come they'll fan out and spread themselves harmlessly. It was for that the old sea wall was built."

"There's no hurry," said Roddy Hernon sharply. "It's

twenty-nine years between those big waves. We can take a few years to think it over."

"They often come in cycles," said Mr. Lynch as if he were talking about something rather uninteresting. "You might have one every year now, for a few years."

"How clever he is!" said Mike Fagan. "How does he know what the sea will do? Sure, no one knows that. If we knew it ourselves, we'd be millionaires long since."

Suddenly James Donnelly raised his voice:

"Men of Inisharcain, are you all fools? Can't you see that this man is talking sense? If we don't do as he says, we'll lose everything we have in the world—"

The same voice from the back, that had offered to scuttle the boat, said derisively:

"Sure, 'tis true for you, Jamesy. You'd lose all your fine barrels and bags. 'Tis a big thing for your place when a wave comes."

The men all laughed at this because no one ever likes the man who takes their money, even if he gives good value in return. Encouraged, Roddy spoke more sharply:

"Just hand up those boys. We'll know what to do with them."

Then Sally's voice rang out:

"Women of Inisharcain! No one is asking you what you think. Do you want to go through the same torment again that you had this year? Do you want to have filthy walls, and drowned featherbeds and pillows and blankets, and broken china that it will take two years of egg-money to buy new? Do you want to have your hens and your little pigs drowned, and maybe your children too the next time? Or will you let this decent engineering man come ashore and do what he's paid to do, and what God gave him the brains to do, God bless him? Which do you want?"

During this speech, the men had growled a lot among themselves, but they were silenced by the encouraging yelps of the women while Sally recited the list of what they had suffered from the big wave. Now, at her last question, all of the women called out:

"The wall! The sea wall mended!"

"Why should we sit waiting for misfortune?"

"Come ashore, decent man."

"And only for the boys, we'd never see an engineer at all."

" 'Tis true, they're great boys."

"Men have no sense, after all."

Shuffling and jostling, they pushed to the edge of the quay and helped Mr. Lynch ashore. After him, much more timidly, came Pat and John. The women made a half-circle behind them and escorted them up the quay as far as Sally's house. As they moved off, they heard Mike Fagan say in a resigned tone to the pilot and his mate:

"Ye may as well tie up the boat so, and come on up to our place and we'll see is there e'er an old drop in the bottle for you."

So leaving a gap of a hundred yards in between, the men followed them.

In those first days, whenever Mr. Lynch was working at the sea wall with his little bag of instruments, he was watched by a hostile group that leaned on the high wall of the quay, muttering among themselves. But as the days went on, one by one the men began to ask him questions, and to give him advice, until at last one evening three of them dropped into Sally's house after supper for a chat. Then the battle was over. The boys were sitting on the hobs that evening, while Sally hopped around making the tea. Suddenly she stopped and looked sharply at Mr. Lynch, who was sitting in the biggest chair with his long legs tucked in out of the way.

"You look to me like a man that can sing," she said.

Afterwards she told John that she had heard him humming to himself in the mornings while he shaved himself, but she had had no idea of whether he knew any songs.

"I can sing," he said now, quietly.

And without unfolding his legs, nor straightening himself up in any way, he begun on "Boulavogue." His voice flowed out so easily one hardly knew when it began or ended. At the second verse, one of the men got up and went outside. Later Mr. Lynch told Sally that when he saw this happen he feared that he had made a mistake, and that the men would go away one by one. What happened was the reverse. After "Boulavogue" he sang "The Rising of the Moon," and in the middle of this, the man who had gone out came back with three others. Then more and more people began to come in as word went around that the foreign engineer was able to sing. Before the evening was out, the kitchen was full and a crowd stood outside the door as well.

Within a week, the islandmen were singing too, and Sally's kitchen was full every evening, as long as Mr. Lynch stayed. When the time came for him to go, again the quay was crowded for the pilot boat's arrival, but now the crowd was in a very different humor. They handed

him down the steps as carefully as if he were made of glass.

"Come back soon."

"We'll be watching the sea every day, from morning till night."

"We'll have great work in the daytime and great sport in the night time."

The pilot and his mate looked astonished. They kept their mouths shut by force, it seemed, but anyone could see that there would be great questioning as soon as they would be far enough away from the quay not to be heard ashore.

In later times, the months during which the sea wall was being repaired seemed like one long, wonderful party. The day's work seemed to give the men an appetite for music. Supper would be barely over when the first visitors would appear at Sally's door, and often at midnight she had to say:

"Now, men! That's enough for one night. Off home with you and we'll have more tomorrow."

The new sea wall was ready before the heavy seas of winter began to batter it. Then, one afternoon in December, when a westerly gale was blowing, another big wave came. This time everyone saw it. At all the doors where there was a view of the sea, a little group stood watching. No one ran. No one moved. Along came the wave, prancing, with its tip curled over like a feather. Closer and closer it came. When it reached the sea wall, it lowered its head and began to crawl out sideways, looking, it seemed, for an easy way around the island.

Now everyone began to chatter together.

"It's a fine job, for sure. It's a pity Mr. Lynch wasn't here to see that wave going off with itself."

"Now we can sleep at nights and not be afraid of waking up to find our beds in the tide."

"There's no need for starting the new house," said Jim Connor, who had put off his building until he would see how the new wall would serve. And he said: "Sally has the right sense, and she had the experience from her James, God rest him. There's wisdom in age, so there is."

" 'Tis true, 'tis true," said all the people.

Sally listened quietly to this but when she was alone with the boys she said drily:

"We mended more than the sea wall, I'm thinking." Suddenly there were tears in her eyes. "I'll tell you something now that I never told to anyone before. Ever since the first wave came, the fear is on me that I wouldn't die here in my own house, that I'd have to move away up to a safer place and that all the little things I know since I was born would be buried under the sea. Isn't that a queer notion? You'd say an old woman that's well past seventy years should have more sense. It's a funny thing that when I was young and strong, I'd have gone around the world for sport and I'd never have given a thought to where I'd lay my bones in the latter end. There's the old wish that you often hear: Long life to you, and death in Ireland. Death in my own house I wanted, and now I'll have my wish."

And this, more than anything else, made it seem that all they had suffered had been well worth while.